Siren

A Kate Redman Mystery: Book 9

Celina Grace

This book is for my husband Chris, with my love and thanks for that long car journey where we worked out the plot. ☺

Prologue

THE MOST SOUGHT-AFTER PROPERTY IN the West Country town of Abbeyford lay in what was known as The Old Town; a small collection of ancient buildings, situated within a half-mile square area. There, one could find the remains of the fifteenth century monastery that gave the town its name, the old Corn Exchange that sat on the edge of the original town square, and the few streets of Tudor buildings that lined the roads that radiated off from the square itself. The streets were cobbled, the houses timbered, with small, many-paned windows and doorways that a man of average height would find difficult to enter without banging his head.

Mia Farraday was the lucky owner of one of those very houses, along with her husband Simon. She picked her way across the cobbles in her heels, knowing from experience that to hurry across them was to court a sprained ankle or worse. She carried a Cath Kidston oilcloth handbag in one hand and a furled umbrella in the other, because the morning's sunshine was already being threatened by looming black clouds. Mia reached the comparative safety of the pavement, where cobbles gave way to flagstones, and reached into her bag for the keys to the house. Both she and Simon used the house as a temporary office, as well as renting it out as a holiday home, and Mia was there today to retrieve a file she'd left behind the last time she'd been there.

The front door was painted black, with a shiny brass doorknocker affixed to the wood, and the number of the house beneath it. Mia pushed open the front door and entered the tiny hallway. She was a small woman, but even she ducked her head a little to be sure of clearing the lintel. She shut the front door behind her, clicked on the hallway light, and put down her handbag.

Straightening up, she caught sight of herself in the mirror that hung on the wall by the door. Afterwards, she was to marvel at how carefree she looked then, how remarkably calm and relaxed. But then, that was the last moment, almost the very last moment of what she was later to think of as 'Before'. It was the moment where her life remained as yet unchanged, all the trauma and the horror to come in the future, the 'After'.

Smiling a little, Mia turned away from the mirror and began to climb the steep, narrow stairs. The house itself was very small; a drawing room downstairs, along with a kitchen, and behind the house, a courtyard garden. Upstairs, on two further floors, were two bedrooms, one so tiny as to almost be called a box room and a bathroom converted from one of the other original bedrooms. Mia remembered that she'd left that particular file in the main bedroom. By the bed it had been, hadn't it? She reached the upstairs landing and pushed open the door, humming a tune she'd heard on the radio that morning.

The room was in darkness, both blinds and the curtains drawn at the window. Mia stopped at the entrance to the room, the hum dying on her lips. The room was close, slightly stuffy, and there was a smell in the air, something that reminded her briefly of the food waste bin at home, when it hadn't been emptied for a while. She hesitated, standing in the doorway, and then reached out to snap on the main overhead light.

There was something on the bed, incongruous against the white linen sheets, a black mass of rubber and leather and cord. Breathing hard, Mia took in the shape of the person beneath the dark covering, the dark spattering against the white pillow cases, reddish-brown spots and splashes that had flown all over the bedclothes, and up the pale cream paint of the wall behind the headboard. Heart thudding, she looked and saw the shape of the head behind the leather mask, crushed in like an empty eggshell. The hands, anonymous behind black leather gloves, were handcuffed to the top rail of the bed.

Mia didn't scream. Instead, she backed out of the room slowly until the landing wall arrested her progress. The strength ran out of her legs just as quickly as if someone had scythed them out from under her, and she thumped down on the floor at the top of the stairs. She reached for her phone with hands shaking so much she could scarcely grasp it. It took three attempts to hit the right icons on the screen and as she waited for the operator to answer, she remembered how she'd looked in the mirror downstairs, just those few minutes ago, and how she would probably never look that way again. Not now, because that was how she had looked Before. And now, it was After.

Chapter One

DETECTIVE INSPECTOR MARK OLBECK WRUNG his hands. Actually wrung them. Kate Redman looked at him quizzically for a moment and then gently poked him in the side. They were both sitting in Olbeck's car.

"Why are you doing that with your hands?"

Olbeck looked sheepish. "I'm just nervous, I guess."

"Aw." Kate gave his arm a squeeze. "You do know this is just a preliminary chat, don't you? You're not actually going to meet any of the kids this time?"

"I know *that*. I'm still nervous."

"You'll be fine. Should we go in?"

Olbeck squeezed his eyes closed for a moment, blowing his cheeks outward on a puff of breath. "I wish Jeff were here."

"I know," said Kate. "I'm not much of a substitute."

"Oh, I didn't mean that, Kate – God, I'm glad you're here. Really glad. It's just – it'll be me and Jeff hopefully actually doing this together. I just wish he could be here from the start, that's all."

"I know," Kate said again. She squeezed his arm once more. "He won't miss out on any of the important bits, you know."

"You're right," Olbeck said in a decisive tone. He pulled the keys from the engine and put them in his coat pocket. "Let's go in."

Kate and Olbeck got out of the car and began to walk towards the open door of the community centre. Kate could see the sign taped to the door as they approached it. *Abbeyford Fostering and Adoption Group Information Evening*, she read, as they walked into the entrance hall.

"By the way," Olbeck said suddenly, as they approached the inner set of double doors. "Don't think I'm not aware of what this must be like for you. I really appreciate you coming along and giving me some moral support, Kate. *Really* appreciate it."

"Oh, don't be daft," Kate said, and gave him a friendly nudge with her elbow. "That's what friends are for."

She was the one who pushed open the doors, Olbeck following closely behind her. There were a few people standing about, a table full of leaflets and clipboards to one side and about twenty chairs arranged in a circle. A woman spotted them standing rather hesitantly by the doors and came over to them, a welcoming smile on her face.

"Hello there, I'm Janet. Have we got you down as registered?"

Olbeck nodded. "I'm Mark Olbeck – I think we spoke on the phone earlier?"

"Oh, Mark, yes, of course. The policeman, isn't it?" Janet took a look at the paper she held in one hand, obviously a list of names. Then she looked at Kate with slight puzzlement. "So, you must be...Jeff?"

Kate chuckled. "No, I'm Kate. Just a friend, coming along for support."

They all laughed at the mistake. "Jeff's in the States on a lecture tour at the moment—" Olbeck began, before his mobile phone began to ring incessantly from the inner pocket of his jacket. "Sorry, Janet, would you excuse me?" He ducked away a little, just as Kate's own phone began to ring as well.

"Sorry," Kate mumbled, seeing everyone in the room begin to look over in what looked like disapproval. She followed Olbeck from the room, lifting the phone to her ear.

"Kate, mate," Theo's voice said into her ear. "You with Mark?"

"Yes. Was that Anderton ringing him just now?"

"Yup. You both need to come in. We've got a pretty nasty case here."

Kate glanced across to Olbeck, who met her gaze with a grimace. She could tell from the disappointment on his face that he was well aware that they wouldn't be attending the fostering and adoption information session that evening. She rolled her eyes in a way she hoped was suitably sympathetic.

Theo was talking, telling her about the body found; tied to a bed, bound and gagged with significant head injuries. Kate listened without saying much, conscious of the fact there were several people almost within earshot.

"Where are we meeting you?" she asked Theo as his briefing came to a close, feeling a not altogether unpleasant feeling of tension in the pit of her stomach. She noted the address details that Theo gave her and mentally raised her eyebrows. The Old Town was not an area associated with crime, let alone violent death.

Saying goodbye, she looked up to see Olbeck putting away his own phone with a purposeful look. "Was that Theo?" he asked.

"Yep. We're heading for Old Town, right?"

"Right." Olbeck looked back towards the hall and sighed. "I'd better go and make my excuses to Janet."

"Never mind." Kate tried to sound both sympathetic and reassuring. "There'll be other meetings. I'll meet you back at the car."

*

IN THE CAR, WITH OLBECK driving towards the address that Theo had given, Kate asked if there had been an identification yet.

"Yes, there has. Didn't Theo tell you?" Kate shook her head. "The victim's wife identified him. Well, she *found* him, poor woman. His name was Simon Farraday, fifty-three years old, local businessman."

"So do we have any theories yet?"

It was Olbeck's turn to shake his head. "Murder by person or persons unknown, that's all that Anderton had, so far. Ah, here we are."

They circled Market Square, where the house was located, rather pointlessly. Blue and white crime scene tape blocked off the doorway and the pavements nearby were packed with uniformed and non-uniformed officers, SOCOs, and a small but rapidly growing phalanx of press journalists and photographers being reluctantly held at bay. Olbeck had to stop the car and reverse carefully down the narrow street until they could join the main road.

"Come on," Kate said, in affectionate exasperation. "You can't get a parking space there at the best of times, let alone when there's just been a murder."

"I know. I wasn't thinking properly." Olbeck dived triumphantly into a space at the curb as another car pulled out. "Right, let's get in there and see what's happening."

*

THE ENTRANCE HALL TO THE house was very small and seemed even smaller with the amount of white-coated people milling about and moving through it. Kate and Olbeck suited up in the little tent that had been hastily erected on the pavement directly outside the front door and stepped through. The stairs beyond were steep and narrow and the ceiling low enough even for Kate to worry about bumping her head. They climbed upwards, cautiously, emerging into a slightly more spacious hallway on the first floor. Looking up, Kate saw Detective Chief Inspector Anderton's head emerge from over the staircase railings on the next floor up and he shouted down to them to keep climbing.

Kate had attended many crime scenes, and some had been more difficult to bear than others. As she walked up the final set of stairs to emerge onto the landing, and to look into the bedroom beyond, she could smell that distinctive metallic scent in the air. It was the scent of blood that was, even at this early stage, beginning to decay. She licked her lips nervously, bracing herself for the sight of the body. She was reminded of the horror-film scene of a case involving a multiple murder, several years ago now. But it wouldn't be that bad, would it? There was just one victim here, after all.

She and Olbeck moved around to the doorway of the bedroom and looked in. Kate let out her breath in a short puff, half relief and half shock. It wasn't the blood so much – as crime scenes go, Kate had definitely seen worse. What was a shock was the body itself. They'd arrived so early that the body was still as it had been when it had been discovered: handcuffed to the top rail of the bed and dressed head to foot in black leather. Even the face was covered, save for a slit that presumably hid the mouth. The outline of the skull beneath the black leather looked like the shell of an egg that had been tapped too hard with a spoon.

Breathing shallowly, Kate stood for a moment with Olbeck, taking in the scene. She had a fleeting moment of wondering how exactly he would take to this type of thing once he became a father. A moment later, she was chastising herself for that thought. Hadn't she once been a mother, if only for a short time? Did it really make any difference?

Shaking off those thoughts, she looked up at her friend. "What do you think?"

Olbeck frowned. He wasn't squeamish, thought Kate, but he was sensitive. That was partly what made him such an excellent detective. "Does that mask thing look like it's been moved?"

"What do you mean?"

Olbeck stepped closer to the body. Up close, it looked even less human than it had appeared from the doorway. Just a lifeless black-clad dummy, a mannequin, a leather scarecrow. "I mean, it looks as though someone's lifted it up a bit. Doesn't it?"

Kate bent forward to look more closely. As she did, there was a minor scrimmage outside in the corridor and then the milling crowds of forensic workers parted to let through a welcome addition to the scrum. Detective Sergeant Chloe Wapping's blonde head came into view, and at the sight of Kate she broke into a smile, quickly subdued as she took in the scene.

"Bird," she said, coming up to stand next to Kate.

"Bird," said Kate, concealing her own grin. She didn't know why Chloe and she had started using this absurd greeting, but it seemed to have settled into a tradition that always made her smile.

Olbeck rolled his eyes. "Is this really the time?"

"Oh, go on with you," Chloe said, giving him an irreverent dig in the ribs. "Besides, that poor bugger doesn't mind, he's past feeling anything. Poor sod."

All three of them regarded the body once more. The initial shock was over, and now Kate could feel the usual calmness of her professionalism settling over her. She almost snuggled into it, as if into a comfort blanket. Looking quite dispassionately at the body by now, she noted the handcuffs that fastened the wrists to the brass headrail of the bed. The cuffs themselves were decorated with a jarringly frivolous strip of pink marabou feathers. The feathers on both cuffs were stiffened with blood, dried into hard little clumps.

Chloe leaned in so she could murmur into Kate's ear. "I know I may be jumping to some rather sexist conclusions, but is it likely that a man would use those sort of handcuffs? With another man, I mean?"

As one, the two of them looked across at Olbeck, who snorted. "I'm bloody *gay*, not a sadomasochist. Why would I know?"

"Alright, sorry." Kate patted his arm. "Surely if we have an identification, we'll know more about his sexual orientation by now, even if it's relevant.

Anyway, I thought he was married? Didn't his wife find him?"

As if he'd overheard her, Anderton made his way through the crowd towards them. "This house is owned by the Farradays, Simon and Mia. They use it as a holiday let and sometimes as a temporary office for Simon Farraday's business." He'd reached the three of them by now and looked over at the body. "His wife had no idea he'd be here, apparently. She thought he was on a work trip to Cheltenham."

A silence fell, as much as silence could in that bustling room. Kate, observing the body again, frowned. "Hang on a minute, you said his wife identified him, correct?"

"Right," said Anderton.

"Well, *how*? His face is completely covered. How did she recognise him?"

Chloe's face twitched in what could have been disgust or amusement. "Perhaps she recognised the leather outfit. Maybe she's into all this, too."

Anderton looked as if he weren't amused. "No, she identified him because she pulled that mask up to have a look at his face." Shocked, the three other police officers turned to him. "Yes, I know, I know. And don't worry, she's under enough suspicion as it is, being his wife."

"So, when can we—" Kate began, but Anderton shook his head.

"She's not in any fit state to be questioned, yet,"

he said. "I thought for one moment, when we first got here, she'd have to be sedated."

"Where is she now?" asked Chloe.

"Back at the Farradays' main residence, with Rav and a few family liaison officers." Anderton looked at his watch. "The pathologist should be here soon, so I suggest we reconvene somewhere less crowded and take it from there."

He stood back to let the others leave the room before him. Kate took a single look back as she passed through the doorway. Even knowing the victim's identity didn't make the body look any less…unearthly. Unusually for her, she had to repress a shiver as she looked and then turned her head away.

Chapter Two

THEY WALKED DOWN THE STAIRS in single file, unable to do otherwise due to the narrowness of the staircase. Kate was last but one, with Anderton bringing up the rear. She had to walk down quite awkwardly, as he was talking to her all the way down to the ground floor, telling her to expect some media attention. Kate found she had to twist her neck uncomfortably to be able to hear what he was saying above the clatter of their feet on the stairs.

"—bound to be high profile, given the manner of his death and who he was," Anderton was saying.

Thankfully, Kate had reached the ground floor. "You knew him, then?"

"I knew *of* him. I didn't know him personally. He was quite a high-profile business man around here. Fingers in a few political pies, as well."

"In what way?" asked Olbeck, who was waiting for them at the front door. Chloe had already gone outside. Kate could hear her snapping, "No comment" to the waiting photographers.

"He was an ex-councillor. Tory, obviously. He stood down at the last election but he threw a lot of money behind the general election campaign."

Kate nodded. Abbeyford had been a solidly held Liberal Democrat seat for fifteen years, before the forming of the coalition government. The subsequent crushing election defeat of that party had meant Abbeyford now had a Conservative Member of Parliament.

Just as they were preparing for the onslaught of camera flashes outside, the door opened to admit another welcome face, one that Kate wasn't expecting.

"Hi, Kirsten," Kate exclaimed. Doctor Kirsten Telling was an old acquaintance of the team and had been on maternity leave for the past year. This was the first time Kate has seen her back at work, hence her rather enthusiastic welcome.

Kirsten Telling, one of the local pathologists, greeted all of the officers in her usual quiet manner. She smiled particularly at Kate; the two women had always got on well. Kate opened her mouth to enquire about Peter, Kirsten's ten-month old son, and then shut it again. Asking after a baby felt entirely inappropriate, given the setting.

"Morning, Doctor." Anderton squeezed back against the wall to let Kirsten past. "We'll let you get on with things."

"Will one of you be staying?"

Anderton looked doubtful. "It's a hell of a

squeeze up there, particularly with all the SOCOs milling around."

"I can pop back in an hour," Kate suggested. "Then we can get the preliminaries but I won't be in your way."

"Very well." Kirsten gave her small, reserved smile once more as she tucked her hair inside a plastic cap. "I'll look forward to seeing you then, Kate."

"See you then."

"Come on then, troops," said Anderton. "Brace yourselves and get your 'no comments' at the ready."

Olbeck and Kate did as they were told, and Anderton pushed open the front door to a rising crescendo of whirrs and clicks as the waiting cameras outside sprang into action.

*

IN THE ABSENCE OF ANY private space not overlooked by flashing cameras or gawking onlookers, the four of them climbed into the back of one of the police vans parked at the edge of the square. There, the three officers crouched awkwardly on the hard plastic seats and looked expectantly towards their boss.

"Now," Anderton said. "Let's make this quick, before our arses die completely. Mark, can you take Chloe and head back to the office, pull up everything you can on Simon Farraday, see how Theo's getting on with witness reports, CCTV and anything else you can think of?"

"No problem," Olbeck said, and Chloe nodded her agreement.

"Good," said Anderton. "Right, Kate, you're with me." Kate had time to feel a tiny jab of surprise – she normally worked with Olbeck or with Chloe, now the ex-Salterton officer had joined the Abbeyford team.

"Where are we going?" she asked.

"*Chez* Farraday, to see if our prime witness and possible suspect, Mia Farraday, has recovered enough to be questioned yet." Kate said nothing but raised her eyebrows in a sort of rueful, questioning manner. She wondered silently to herself whether this might actually be one of those cases that *looked* complicated, on first impressions, but was actually very straightforward. If Simon Farraday's wife had killed him, it could all be over by teatime.

Chance would be a fine thing. As they clambered awkwardly out of the back of the van, she said goodbye to her team mates and followed Anderton to his car, which was parked two streets away. As a senior officer, he warranted a driver but never used one, always preferring to drive himself. This meant that Kate sat up next to him, rather than being relegated to the back seat. She felt a twinge of uneasiness, and something else, as she climbed into the front seat. It had been a while since she had been alone with her boss.

"Where do the Farradays live, sir?" she asked as Anderton drove off, trying to clip her aura of professionalism back around her.

Anderton gestured towards the satellite navigation system on the windscreen. "Somewhere near Cudston Magna. Got some great big pile right out in the countryside."

"What kind of business was he in?"

Anderton slowly negotiated his way out of the complicated system of narrow one-way streets that wound through the Old Town and hesitated before answering. "Not entirely sure of that. Some kind of business to business thing. He was an entrepreneur all the way from school, inherited his father's property business, sold that for millions about twenty years ago and founded this current concern, the details of which escape me for the moment."

"So, he's rich, then?" Kate pondered on the other rich men she'd met in the course of her career. Stelios and Yanis Costa, Michael Dekker, Jack Dorsey and Alex Hargreaves...none of them had used their money as an ethical force for good. Had Simon Farraday been like them? What had he been like? A good man, a bad man or, like most men, something in-between?

No doubt his wife could shed some light on his personality. Kate found herself hoping that the woman had recovered enough by now to talk to them.

They drove through picturesque countryside, always looking its best at this time of the year. The hedgerows were beginning to mist over in pale green as fresh leaves unfolded in the spring sunshine. Bluebells, late daffodils and the tiny white stars of daisies dotted the fields and embankments. As they swung around a corner, Kate closed her eyes momentarily against the dazzle of the sunshine.

Anderton glanced over at her. "How's young Tin doing?"

Kate's eyes snapped open. For some reason best known to himself, Anderton always referred to Kate's boyfriend Tin as 'young Tin', despite the fact that the journalist currently working abroad in New York was well into his forties. It always irritated Kate, but of course, now as ever, she made no mention of it to her boss.

"He's fine," she said.

"When do you go out there for your visit?"

"At the end of April." That was in just over a week. Kate hoped that the investigation wouldn't take such a serious turn as to stop her from taking her much anticipated time off. No, surely it wouldn't? She hadn't seen her boyfriend for nearly three months, since she kissed him goodbye at the airport.

"Have you been to New York before?"

Kate shook her head. "No, I've never even been to America before." She didn't mention that her family had never been able to afford overseas holidays – or, indeed, any holidays at all.

"Great place," Anderton said, glancing at the sat nav screen and then flicking on the indicator. "Was out there myself about five years ago—"

Whatever he had been trying to say died away

20

as he negotiated a narrow bend in the road. The car had turned into a driveway flanked by two massive wooden posts and an equally imposing wooden gate, stained black. The driveway was tarmacked and it was a smooth, sweeping ride through sun-dappled woodland. At one point, Kate spotted a drift of bluebells where the azure of the flowers was so intense, for a moment she thought she was looking at a woodland lake reflecting the sky.

When the driveway ended in front of the Farradays' house, the contrast was jarring. The house was almost aggressively modern, square, boxy and multi-levelled, its frontage a mixture of cedar cladding, black glass, steel and stone. A short walkway led to the front door, a shallow water feature running along either side. Kate wondered briefly if either of the Farradays had ever fallen in, perhaps missing their footing on a dark night or coming home a bit tipsy.

"Nice place" Anderton said briefly, parking the car. Kate gave him a disbelieving glance but said nothing.

A family liaison officer opened the door to them. Kate recognised her face without being able to put a name to it. They exchanged suitably sombre smiles and the officer led them through a stone-flagged, cavernous hallway, through a kitchen more suited in size and fittings to one made for industrial catering, and finally into a massive dining cum living area, big enough to comfortably accommodate three enormous modular sofas, a six-foot-wide coffee table and a dining table that could have easily seated fifteen people. Kate wondered whether the Farradays had a large family. Perhaps they liked entertaining a lot?

A woman who had to be Mia Farraday was hunched forward on one of the giant sofas. She was a thin, dark woman with a pretty, sharp-featured face and very blue eyes. Kate recognised in her the physical type she herself belonged to. Irish forebears, perhaps? The most immediate impression she had was of a woman in the grip of profound and unrelenting shock. Mia was visibly shaking, and if her teeth weren't chattering, that was probably because her hand was pressed firmly against her mouth.

Kate and Anderton took a seat opposite Mia Farraday. She hadn't spared them so much as a glance since they came in. Her eyes, wide and aghast, were fixed firmly on the floor. Kate felt her natural suspicion of the murder victim's wife fading. That kind of distress and upset was very hard to fake.

Anderton began with the usual words of condolence. "Are you feeling up to talking to us, Mrs Farraday? Any information you can give us will be very useful in our investigation."

For a moment, Kate thought the woman wasn't going to answer. Then Mia gave a tiny nod and sat up a little, bringing her hand away from her mouth. Kate saw that she'd actually bitten through her lip – blood was smeared across it. The family officer noticed too and brought forward a tissue which she held out to

Mia. Mia stared, uncomprehending for a moment and then took it and dabbed it against the wound.

"If you could just talk us through what happened this morning, Mrs Farraday," Anderton asked. "In your own words and taking your time. Take as much time as you want."

When Mia spoke, her voice was husky, whether through tears or by nature, it wasn't apparent. "I – I had to go to the house to get some paperwork. We let it out as a holiday let and we have some guests coming this weekend, so I needed to – to check a few things."

She stopped talking and they all waited for a minute, before Anderton prompted her gently. "You had no idea of your husband being there?"

Mia shook her head. Kate saw a tear fly out from the corner of her eye and hit the glossy surface of the coffee table. "No. No, I had no idea. He was supposed to be at a conference in Cheltenham. I wasn't expecting him back until late tonight." She closed her eyes and took a deep breath. "I unlocked the front door and went inside. Nothing was – I didn't notice anything wrong then. The paperwork's kept upstairs in the main bedroom, in the desk, so I went up there..."

Again she trailed off, her eyelids fluttering. Then she seemed to pull herself together.

"I – I could smell something odd. Sweetish but not a nice smell. I suppose I opened the door a bit warily and then I – then I saw him—" For a moment Kate thought she was going to break down again, but

Mia seemed to draw on some inner core of strength. Her mouth twisted but she said, "I could see there was someone on the bed, all dressed in black, black leather. There was blood on the pillows."

She lapsed back into silence. Kate saw her clench her shaking hands.

"What happened then, Mrs Farraday?" Anderton asked quietly.

Mia drew her breath in on a shuddering gasp. "I didn't – I didn't think it was Simon. Not then. Why would I? I didn't know who it was. I was in shock – I wasn't thinking. I – I sort of fell backwards into the hallway and got my phone—" She put her thin hands up to her eyes, wiping the tears away. "After I'd phoned the ambulance, I – I went back in—" She looked at the officers with a kind of wincing plea on her face. "I went back and pulled the mask up to see who it was. I shouldn't have touched him, I know that. I'm sorry."

Anderton waved a hand. "Don't worry about that now, Mrs Farraday. Just go on with what happened."

Mia gulped. "I saw it was Simon. I don't know – I was so – I was so *shocked*; I wasn't really thinking anything. I – I don't remember much about what happened next. I think I fell down again. What happened then, I can't really remember."

Kate glanced down at her notes. The nine-nine-nine call from Mia's phone had been put through to the emergency services at seventeen minutes past ten o'clock. Kate made a mental note to get hold of the transcript of that call.

She looked up to see that Anderton was looking at her intently. She raised her eyebrows in response.

"Could you give us a minute, Mrs Farraday?" Anderton got up and ushered Kate out of earshot.

"What's up?"

"Could you ring and find out if we've got a time of death yet? We won't be able to eliminate Mrs Farraday as a suspect until we have that."

Kate had realised that just as Anderton had. "Leave it with me."

She managed to get through to Kirsten Telling after only a few minutes. She listened to her answer, pressed for further clarification (a hopeless task – Kate knew from experience that doctors did not like to pin their colours to the mast too early) and then headed back to Anderton. She didn't say anything but let him read the notes she'd written on her notebook.

"Hmm. Thanks, DS Redman." Kate sat back down again and Anderton turned back to Mia Farraday. "Now, Mrs Farraday, we'll be able to leave you in peace in just a moment but there's just a few other questions we need to ask. Could you tell me what you were doing last night?"

If Mia Farraday recognised this as an attempt to test an alibi, she gave no sign. She wiped her eyes with a white cotton handkerchief – Kate hadn't seen anyone use a real handkerchief in years – and said in a low, tear-choked voice, "I had dinner with the children and Sarah – she's our nanny. That was about six-thirty. I don't normally eat that early but I had to go out, I was due at a friend's house that evening."

"You spent the evening with a friend?" checked Anderton.

Mia tucked the handkerchief up the sleeve of her grey cashmere jumper. "Yes, I spent most of the evening there. I got home about – oh, it must have been after midnight. Perhaps half past twelve."

"Who is this friend, Mrs Farraday?"

"Dorothy Smelton. You might have heard of her, she's the deputy leader of the council."

Kate had heard of Dorothy Smelton and so, from the look on his face, had Anderton. "Yes, I know Councillor Smelton quite well. So you were at her place last night from when exactly to midnight?"

Mia brushed her hair back from her face. She looked white with exhaustion. "I think I left here about seven. It's not far to Dorothy's house, about a twenty-minute drive, so I must have arrived there about seven thirty."

Kate was busy scribbling all this down. She didn't mention it to Anderton but was thinking it would be the work of a moment to confirm these timings with Councillor Smelton. She looked at the time of death that Kirsten Telling had given her. Between ten thirty and eleven thirty pm. If it was the case that Mia

Farraday hadn't left her friend's house until midnight last night, she was cleared.

She sat back a little, listening to Anderton talk. Her gaze fell on a silver-framed photograph on the mantelpiece over the massive modern fireplace, a wedding photograph of a much younger Mia and Simon Farraday, posed on the steps of a church. She wondered about Simon Farraday. He had had a relatively young and attractive wife but, from the look of things, had been waiting for someone else, someone with whom to indulge his more exotic sexual fantasies. Or had he? Was the leather and bondage gear a smokescreen? Had the lover he'd been waiting for killed him? Why? Or had it not been like that at all?

This case is not going to be straightforward, Kate thought with an inner sigh, and then she dismissed those thoughts and turned her attention back to the job in hand.

Chapter Three

KATE MANAGED TO MAKE IT back to the crime scene just as Kirsten Telling was preparing to leave. The doctor was packing the last of her instruments away in her black leather case when Kate came panting through the door of the bedroom, her thighs aching from the steep climb up the staircase. The body of Simon Farraday had been removed, and the Scene of Crime Officers were still hard at work, gathering all the evidence they could.

"Kirsten," Kate said, when she had breath enough to speak. "Anything I can take back for our first debrief? Thanks for the time of death, by the way."

Doctor Telling smiled. She'd put on some weight since the birth of her son but it suited her. She no longer looked quite so unearthly, despite the white-blonde of her hair and the corresponding paleness of her skin. "That really is a ball-park figure, Kate, you know that."

"I know, I know. But you're pretty sure that

he wouldn't have died after eleven thirty? Not after midnight?"

"That's right."

Kate nodded. "Anything else?"

Doctor Telling snapped the locks of her case together. "I'll be doing the post mortem tomorrow, if you want to attend, but I can confirm that, at first glance, he died of severe head injuries." She glanced around the room as if looking for something. "And, if I'm not very much mistaken, SOCO have already bagged up the murder weapon."

"Really?" Kate felt a little caught on the back foot. But then, how was she supposed to have known that? Really, one of the team should have stayed behind, especially now they were working at full capacity, what with Chloe having joined them.

"Yes, it was a candlestick, a metal candlestick. The twin of that one there, I would think." Kate's gaze followed Kirsten's pointing finger, to a small chest of drawers over by the outer wall. A heavy, ornate metal candlestick stood at one end, looking out of place without its matching companion and – if this wasn't too silly a thing to say about an inanimate object – rather forlorn.

"Hmm." Kate rubbed her jaw for a moment, thinking. The fact that the weapon was something already found in the bedroom where the killing had taken place was suggestive. It meant that the killer hadn't brought along a weapon. Did that mean that the murder was not premeditated? But then, what had the motive been? She mentally shook herself. "So, you're saying he was killed by being hit on the head with a candlestick – right?"

Kirsten had packed up her case and was standing politely by Kate, waiting for her to move out of the way of the exit. "Well, on the first pass, that's what it looks like. But we'll know more at the PM."

"Right." Kate stepped aside to let the other woman through. She called after Kirsten, who had disappeared down the staircase. "What time will the PM be tomorrow?"

"I couldn't say for certain yet, Kate. I'll email you later and let you know when I've got a definite time."

"Great. See you then." Kate called a final goodbye and turned back to the bedroom, facing the bloodstained bed.

Simon Farraday had obviously arranged a clandestine meeting with someone here, for kinky sex. Who had it been? A woman? Kate's eyes went to where the fluffy handcuffs had been snapped around the bed frame. They were gone now, bagged and removed as evidence. Would they get any finger prints? Would the candlestick show any? It was pointless speculating, Kate told herself. She would just have to wait for the forensic results.

She walked forward slowly, eyes on the bed. So, what were the possibilities? Had Simon Farraday been handcuffed and then killed, by the woman with whom he was having an affair? Had she, whoever she was, been merely a one-night stand? Had he even been handcuffed willingly? Perhaps the leather and the handcuffs were a smokescreen, a blind – perhaps he'd merely met someone here for an innocent reason and, for whatever motive of their own, they had killed him and then staged the bondage scene? Perhaps his killer hadn't been the woman or the man he'd been meeting for sex? Perhaps there had been more than one killer?

Kate rubbed her temples. The possibilities were beginning to overwhelm her. She made a mental note to check whether there had been any signs of burglary or robbery, remembering a case several years ago where robbery had been the prime motive in what had at first seemed like a sexually-motivated murder case.

With one last lingering glance at the room, she began the slow walk down the steep stairs. From the sounds of it, Mia Farraday's alibi – if Councillor Smelton could confirm it – meant that she was cleared of the murder of her husband. She hadn't seemed a very likely suspect to Kate, as it had been: the crime was an especially violent one, and it was unusual for a woman to murder, especially a well-to-do, middle-class mother. But then, you never knew, did you? Kate reached the front door of the house, braced herself for the flash of the cameras, and let herself out.

*

BY A SMALL MIRACLE, EVERY member of the

Abbeyford CID team was present in the incident room when Kate walked back into the office. Even DCI Anderton himself was there, busily scribbling on the whiteboards that ranged across one of the longer walls. Olbeck stood next to him, every so often pointing out something that Anderton had obviously missed. Chloe, Rav and Theo were gathered around Theo's desk, leaning over and reading from Theo's computer screen. As Kate got closer, she could see they were monitoring the press coverage of the murder.

"Blimey, Chloe, could you have a face any more like a slapped arse?" Theo exclaimed, as footage of a scowling Chloe exiting the Farraday town house was briefly played.

Chloe gave him an annoyed glance. "I hate the press."

Kate had reached her desk by now. Anderton glanced up and saw her. "Ah, Kate, I hope you've got the bare bones for us?"

"As much as I could get, I hope."

"Right, let's not waste any more time. All right, team, gather round. Gather round."

The officers took up their usual briefing positions. Chloe perched herself on the table next to Kate, who sniffed appreciatively. Chloe always wore very nice, expensive perfume and the one she had on today was no exception, a kind of smoky, bittersweet scent. Kate made a mental note to ask her colleague what it was.

"Right," Anderton said, beginning to pace as was

his wont. There was actually a small track worn into the carpet at the front of the room, so many times had he marched up and down it while addressing his team. "The victim, Simon James Farraday. Fifty-three, married with three children. Managing director of Porthos Consultancy Group. High net worth individual, as the bankers like to say. Found by his wife, dead at their holiday let townhouse, this morning." He stopped pacing and swung back in the opposite direction. "I'm assuming all of you will have seen some of the preliminary crime scene photographs, even if you weren't on the scene itself today."

There was a flurry of nods and 'yeses' around the table. Anderton looked over at Kate and raised his eyebrows. "Kate, you've just come from the preliminary medical examination. What was the verdict?"

Kate brushed her fringe out of her eyes. "Death was from multiple head injuries, caused by a heavy metal candlestick, which was actually at the house already—"

Olbeck was grinning. "A *candlestick*? It's too Cluedo for words."

"Professor Plum in the townhouse with a candlestick," Theo said with a snigger.

"All right," Anderton said, quite sharply for him. "Let Kate finish."

Kate finished rolling her eyes at Theo. "*Anyway*, the post mortem's taking place tomorrow – I'm happy

33

to attend that if nobody else is desperate to do it – and we should know more then."

Anderton nodded. "You go, Kate. Report back tomorrow afternoon. Did Kirsten mention the time of death?"

"Yes, and that's important, because she didn't think he'd died after eleven thirty. Certainly not after midnight."

Anderton's thick, grey eyebrows shot up. "Ah, is that so? Well, for those of you who don't know, Simon Farraday's wife, Mia, has a fairly robust alibi for that time. She was spending the evening with her friend, Councillor Dorothy Smelton, who I'm sure you've all heard of. Unless Mrs Farraday has persuaded the good councillor to lie for her, a pretty unlikely turn of events, then that means she's in the clear for the murder."

"Was she ever a prime suspect, guv?" Chloe asked, shifting position on the table and re-crossing her legs. Kate saw Anderton's gaze dip minutely to take in the movement and was surprised at the jab of jealousy that followed. Get a grip, she told herself. It doesn't mean anything, and even if it did, it's nothing to do with you.

Anderton's concentration had only been momentarily jolted by Chloe's long legs. He turned and strode back to the whiteboard, where both the names of Mia Farraday and Simon Farraday were written in black marker pen. "She's the wife, Chloe. Of course she's a suspect. But if that alibi holds – Rav, can you go and confirm it with Councillor Smelton first thing tomorrow, please? – If that alibi holds, then she's in the clear. We can check CCTV as well, see if there's anything to be seen around the square or *en route* to the Farradays' house."

Anderton paused in his pacing, hands on his hips. "Right, what else? Naturally we're waiting for forensic reports to come in. The PM's tomorrow. Theo, make a start on the CCTV in the immediate area of the crime scene. We'll have uniform do a house to house for any pertinent witness statements in the area. Um—" He stopped again, one hand tousling his hair. "We'll need interviews, again with Mia Farraday, her nanny, Rav, you're doing the councillor, Simon Farraday's work colleagues..."

"So, just another day in the mad house then," Theo said, grinning.

"Quite right." Anderton dropped his hand from his head, swung around and headed for the door. "That should be enough to be going on with. I'll be in my office, if anyone needs me."

As was usual, they all sagged a little as the door shut behind him. Chloe looked over at Kate and rolled her eyes. "Blimey. Where do we start?"

"We start with coffee, of course. I'll make it."

As she headed for the little kitchenette area, Kate spared a thought for exactly how much work would ever get done if coffee was ever outlawed. It was a horrible, if not very likely thought. She made a mug for herself and one for Chloe and carried them carefully back over, trying not to spill any.

"Where's mine?" Theo demanded as she handed the brimming mug to Chloe.

"I'm only making coffee for women this week," Kate said, grinning.

Theo snorted. "Tin's been away too long."

Kate poked him. "Don't be stupid."

"Children," Chloe said patiently. "Could we get on?"

"You sound like Anderton," said Kate, smiling, but she sat down obediently and turned her attention to work.

Chapter Four

THE NEXT DAY, KATE OPENED her bedroom curtains to blinding sunlight and a dazzling blue sky. Cheered by the sight, she almost bounded downstairs to prepare her breakfast and feed her cat, Merlin. Her energy was unusual, given the late night she'd had the night before. The Abbeyford team had stayed in the office until way past normal working hours, collating reports, chasing up evidence, telephoning to book appointments with witnesses. It had been almost eleven o'clock at night by the time Kate had returned home. Merlin had been so affronted with her that he'd merely flicked his tail in contempt as she guiltily filled his food bowl. Then Tin had phoned, and they'd talked for almost an hour before Kate had pleaded her early start the next morning and had finally crawled into bed.

Merlin had obviously forgiven her. As Kate munched her wholemeal toast and Marmite, Merlin jumped up onto her lap and curled himself into a comma shape, tail occasionally giving a lazy flick against Kate's leg. She stroked him absentmindedly with her free hand. She was thinking about Tin. Her boyfriend had been in New York for almost three months now, having moved there to take up a foreign correspondent's role for *The Independent*. Kate knew he was expecting her to join him out there at some point. Not for a visit, like the one planned for a week's time, but to actually move there permanently. That was the problem. Kate really didn't know whether she wanted to go or not. She missed Tin – she missed him terribly – but was she going to truncate the career she'd worked so hard for, give up her home and her pet and her friends, and what little left she had of her family, for a man she'd known less than a couple of years?

Frowning, her good mood of the morning dimming, Kate gently pushed Merlin off her lap and went up to clean her teeth and prepare herself fully for the hard day's work ahead.

The bright sunlight was deceptive. Kate stepped outside her front door dressed only in a light jumper and gasped as the cold air struck her. It was *freezing*. Quickly, she grabbed her jacket and hurried to the car. She wondered whether New York would be any warmer when she got there.

She began to automatically take the route towards the police station before she realised with a start that she was due to attend Simon Farraday's postmortem that morning. Quickly, she corrected course but still had to go all the way around the one-way system that bisected the middle of Abbeyford before she could find the right road. Luckily, she was early. Kate was almost always early.

It was Doctor Andrew Stanton who was conducting the autopsy that morning. He was an old boyfriend of Kate's but was now married with his own little boy. Any awkwardness that had once existed between them had long since dissipated. Kate was happy to find that she was actually genuinely pleased to see him.

The body of Simon Farraday had been denuded of all the black leather that had wrapped him like a shroud. It was piled over on one of the other gurneys. Kate wandered over to it as Andrew started up the circular saw. Kate wasn't particularly squeamish, but the screech of the saw as it met bone was never something she relished hearing.

"Can I have a closer look at this?" she shouted over the noise.

Andrew didn't look up, concentrating as he was on his task but he nodded and then shouted confirmation. "Just glove up, obviously."

Kate snapped on a pair of surgical gloves and began to cautiously pick through the pile of leather. She wasn't exactly sure what she was looking for. A manufacturer's label? Something that might help them track down Simon Farraday's mysterious visitor? The leather was heavy, the mask that had covered the face and head stiffened with dried blood.

The whole lot stank, of old sweat, blood and other, less identifiable bodily fluids. Kate found herself making a face. There were no labels in the clothing, anyway – there had been once, but someone had cut them away so only a few threads remained. Was that significant? Or had the labels just tickled or chafed so that they had to be removed for comfort? Kate found herself inwardly smiling at that thought. People didn't put on a bondage suit for *comfort*. She found her mind turning towards an image half amusing, half horrifying – a bondage suit that was shaped like a soft, baggy tracksuit...

"What *are* you grinning about?"

The noise of the saw had stopped and Kate turned around to see Andrew up to his elbows in the chest cavity. She averted her eyes. "Sorry. Just had a funny thought."

"Want to share?"

Kate shook her head. "Not really. Not really appropriate in this setting."

Andrew wasn't really concentrating on her answer. "Mmm, I see." He turned his attention back to the body, and Kate pulled off the surgical gloves, dumped them in the appropriate waste bin, and found a seat over at the side of the room.

The examination proceeded mostly in calm silence, Andrew's terse comments occasionally punctuating the quiet. He had a rather abrupt way of working that was at odds with the warm, friendly man he was at times outside of the examination room. Kate listened and nodded as he spoke.

"Death was due to catastrophic head injuries – blunt force trauma – high blood alcohol content, I can tell just from the smell but we'll have to wait for the toxicity tests, that could take a while – some white powdery residue inside the nostrils, could be cocaine. Again, the tests should show anything untoward – in reasonably good shape for his age, some subcutaneous fat around the waist but muscle tone is high for his age, I'd say he was a regular gym goer – decent teeth, he's had some expensive work done – a vasectomy, I'd say in the past year or so—"

Kate listened and made notes as all of this was mentioned over the course of the examination. She asked again for a definite time of death.

"What did Kirsten say?" Andrew asked. They'd all known each other for so long now that none of them bothered with titles any more. "Half eleven at the latest? Yes, I'd say that was right. Given the lividity, the establishment of rigor, yes, I'd say that was correct."

"So, midnight would be too late, right?" Kate made a mental note to check with Rav whether Councillor Smelton had confirmed Mia Farraday's alibi.

"That's correct."

"Okay, thanks." Kate thought of something else. "Is there, erm, any traces of somebody else? Any other bodily fluids?"

Andrew looked amused. "Not at first glance. He

hadn't ejaculated and the swabs from the outside of the leather, or indeed from his genital area don't show any signs of vaginal fluid. Or indeed, somebody else's sperm."

"Right." Kate stared ahead for a moment, perplexed. If Simon Farraday had been meeting someone else for sex, then clearly it hadn't yet happened when the murder was committed. So did that mean, as she'd hypothesised before, that the murderer was actually someone different to the person Simon had assumed he was meeting? But why would he get all trussed up without being sure of his lover being there? And was it even possible to handcuff yourself to a bed without outside help?

Kate came back to reality with a start, realising that Andrew was beginning the clean-up of the operation. She busied herself with putting away her notebook, checking her phone for messages – none so far – and reaching for her jacket.

"Oh, by the way," Andrew said, settling a green sheet over the eviscerated body of Simon Farraday. Kate had the fleeting thought that bodies after a post mortem always looked smaller, somehow diminished. "Juliet and I were wondering if you'd like to come over for dinner, sometime. Meet Hamish?"

"Oh, that's kind," said Kate, automatically going to give an excuse. Then she reconsidered. Why not? It wasn't that she had any burning desire to meet Andrew's wife, although the thought of a cuddle with a cute toddler was always going to appeal. But her social life at the moment, with Tin away, was pretty thin and the thought of a home-cooked meal at Andrew's lovely house was actually quite a pleasant thought. "I'd love to, Andrew. When were you thinking?"

Once they'd sorted out the date and the time, Kate made her way back outside into the spring sunshine. It was a little warmer by now, although still very much coat and jacket weather. Kate unlocked her car, got in, and drove off, thinking about what she'd just arranged. If she had been Mrs Stanton, the last thing she would have felt like doing was having a cosy home dinner with one of her husband's ex-girlfriends. I mean, there's no harm in it, thought Kate, secure in the knowledge that any remnant of sexual tension between her and Andrew had long since disappeared. But – was it odd? Perhaps she's just a better person than I am, thought Kate, changing gears rather moodily. It didn't help that she'd have to go on her own. Tin was obviously overseas, and there was no one else, bar Olbeck, that she'd want as her plus one. Should she ask Olbeck? Kate pondered as she drove into the police station car park and made up her mind to ask him. And if he wasn't free, then she'd just have to suck it up and go on her own. Briefly, she considered her friend Stuart but dismissed the thought. She hadn't seen Stuart for months – she had a nasty feeling there was going to be an engagement announcement from him and his girlfriend in the near future – and she wasn't sure how Stuart's other half would take to Kate asking him along to a cosy couples' dinner. She locked her car and marched towards the building, feeling unaccountably cross. Something her friend Hannah had once said to her resurfaced in her memory. *Other people's marriages are totally mysterious.* Well, Hannah – ironically happily married herself for nearly twenty years – was right, there. Not that Kate would know. She passed her security card across the scanner to let herself into the station and let the heavy security door slam shut behind her, blocking out the golden spring sunshine.

Chapter Five

OLBECK WAS IN HIS OFFICE when Kate arrived back in the incident room. He caught sight of her and waved, and she headed over, chucking her jacket over the back of her chair as she passed her desk.

"Got a minute?" she asked.

"I was about to ask you the same question. We're to head on out to Simon Farraday's workplace, see whether his colleagues knew anything that was going on."

"Right now?"

"Yes. Why, have you got something else to do?"

"No, it's just—" Kate stopped, not quite knowing what she was going to say. It would have been nice to have been able to sit down for five minutes, grab a hot drink and check her emails.

"Well, let's get going, then."

Rolling her eyes, Kate went to retrieve her jacket again. She passed Rav, hunched over his keyboard and pounding away at the keys, and remembered her question. "Did you get Mia Farraday's alibi confirmed with the councillor, Rav?"

Rav looked up, distracted. "What? Oh yes, it all checks out. Dorothy Smelton said Mia left about eleven o'clock, normal time for her to leave when she went round, apparently. She seemed quite normal."

"Who? Mia or Dorothy Smelton?"

"Mia, of course." Rav went back to his keyboard bashing. "Dorothy Smelton's dead posh. Posh people are never normal."

Kate couldn't help laughing. She said goodbye, reminding Rav not to hunch over for the sake of his posture, and then hurried for the exit, where Olbeck was just disappearing from sight.

Once in the car, she updated Olbeck on Rav's news.

"Well, that's something," he said. "Although that would have been nice and neat, wouldn't it? We could have had it all wrapped up by now."

"Things are never *that* nice and neat." Kate was pushing at the buttons of the radio, trying to find a decent radio station.

"There's CDs in the glovebox."

"No thanks," Kate said with a wink. "Not with *your* musical tastes."

Olbeck snorted but said nothing. The sky was beginning to cloud over, and Kate relaxed back into the passenger seat, glad of the powerful car heater. She remembered her dinner appointment with the Stantons and asked Olbeck if he'd like to come.

"When? Tomorrow? Oh, sorry, Kate. That's the one night I absolutely cannot do. Jeff and I have got another adoption information session that evening."

Thoughts of the Stantons forgotten, Kate sat up. "Oh. Great. So you're definitely going to go for it, then?"

Olbeck looked both happy and scared. "Yes, I think we actually are. Bloody nerve-wracking."

"You'll be fine." Kate lapsed into silence for a moment, thinking about what he'd said. She never spoke anymore about her own experience of adoption, and she'd had enough therapy by now for it not to be quite such a painful memory as it had been but...there was always a 'but'.

She sensed, rather than saw Olbeck glance over at her. He cleared his throat and she tensed. "Do you ever – do you ever—"

"No," Kate said, cutting him off.

"How did you know what I was going to ask?"

Kate rolled her eyes. "Call it women's intuition."

Olbeck huffed and they drove on in silence for a while. Then he said, "So, what was I going to ask?"

"Look, can we just leave it?"

Olbeck looked over at her again, half smiling, half frowning. "Kate..." Kate raised her eyebrows and he half laughed and said "Okay, okay, we'll leave it."

They drove on, out of Abbeyford and into the countryside, heading for Wallingham, where Simon Farraday's consultancy firm was located. Despite the gloom of the grey clouds gathering above them, the rolling hills and fields looked fresh-minted, in part due to the bright green of the new leaves unfurling on the trees and bushes that lined each side of the road.

"No, I don't think about contacting him," Kate said, so softly she wasn't even sure Olbeck had heard her. He gave no sign that she had spoken, concentrating on the road. "No, I don't think about that at all."

"What was that?"

"Nothing. Doesn't matter." Kate stared out of the window, blinking a little.

*

WALLINGHAM WAS A BIGGER TOWN than Abbeyford, missing out on the title of city only by virtue of the fact that it had no cathedral. Simon Farraday's firm was located right in the middle, in the central business district that abutted the main shopping thoroughfare. Parking, unsurprisingly, was at a premium. Luckily, the Porthos Consultancy Group had its own small car park, and as Olbeck drove in, Kate pointed out that the space marked 'Managing Director' was empty.

Olbeck half laughed. "Well, it would be, wouldn't it?"

"So park there," said Kate. "*He's* not going to care, is he?"

Olbeck gave her a look but rolled the car into the late Simon Farraday's parking space. Kate half expected a scandalised receptionist to come running out from the glass and steel framed entrance hall but she was disappointed. Getting out of the car, she realised the whole building had a strangely empty look about it. The blinds were pulled down at every window, and she could see no sign of anyone behind the reception desk.

"They are actually open, aren't they?" she asked, uncertainty edging her tone.

Olbeck looked a little uneasy. "Yes, they are. I phoned earlier."

They advanced towards the front entrance to the building and then Kate saw a black-suited woman pop up into sight behind the reception desk, rather like a sombre jack-in-the-box.

As they introduced themselves, and handed over their warrant cards for inspection, Kate looked at the woman – girl, rather, she only looked about twenty – for signs of grief. But there was nothing there, no red eyes, no expression of shock. Perhaps the black suit was standard wear for her, rather than an expression of mourning.

While they waited for the deputy managing director of the company, Kate took a short stroll around the reception area. It was standard issue for a high-end business: glossy magazines and freshly folded copies of The Financial Times on the square glass coffee table. Black leather sofas and armchairs. Two large ficus trees in pots, which could have been either high-quality fakes or very well looked after real plants. Safe, expensive, boring. Kate wondered briefly what it was like to work in an office like this. Clock in every day, spend the day sitting at your desk or in meetings, clock out at the end of the day. Do it again day after day, year after year. She repressed a shudder. No thanks. She'd take the bad coffee and the tatty carpet of the incident room any day, over this luxurious but soulless workplace.

A man arrived in the reception area and shook hands with Olbeck. He was much older than Simon Farraday, or looked older: white haired, somewhat stooped and wearing a pair of silver-framed spectacles. Kate went over and was introduced.

"Good morning, DS Redman," said the man, shaking hands. It was more of a brief handclasp than a shake. "I'm Ewan Askell, the deputy managing director. Please, do come this way, we'll go up to my office."

His office turned out to be located on the top floor, four flights up, and next to a much larger, corner office with Simon Farraday's name on the door. Kate and Olbeck exchanged glances.

"We'd like to have a look at Mr Farraday's office once we've finished our chat," Olbeck said to Ewan Askell, who looked a little startled and then nodded, rather nervously.

They seated themselves in Askell's office and the usual pleasantries and words of condolence were exchanged.

"I'm sure I don't have to tell you what an awful shock it was to hear the news." Ewan Askell sat in a shaft of sunlight, and the gleam of it turned the surfaces of his glasses opaque. Was that deliberate? Kate wondered. She made a mental note to ask Olbeck if Askell had an alibi and whether it checked out. They could discuss it on the way back to the station.

"I'm sure it must have been, Mr Askell." Olbeck was long versed in this kind of interview. "We're hoping you might be able to tell us something of Simon Farraday, help us get a handle on the kind of man he was, whether you have any theories as to his death, that sort of thing."

"Me?" Askell sounded surprised, if not aghast. "Theories?"

"Well, you worked with the man for some years, isn't that correct?"

Askell nodded. "Yes, we've been working together almost since the inception of the company. I suppose I did know him *quite* well, but you know what it's like – a working relationship isn't quite the same as a friendship, is it?"

"So you wouldn't say you were friends then? Despite working together for so long?"

Askell sounded awkward. "Well – I suppose – we weren't close. Perhaps that's what I'm trying to say."

"I understand." Olbeck looked down at his notes. Kate knew he was doing it to let the silence drag on a bit, to see if Askell was prompted to add anything more. He remained silent.

"So what can you tell us about Simon Farraday, Mr Askell?" Olbeck appeared to reconsider. "Let's qualify that, it's a bit vague. Would you say you had a good working relationship?"

"I – I suppose so."

"You suppose so?"

"Well, I—" Askell shifted a little in his chair. Kate watched him with slightly narrowed eyes. The man was nervous. More nervous than a visit from the police would warrant? She wondered a little about Ewan Askell. "It's not *that* – it's just that Simon was – well, he had a very strong personality, shall we say. He didn't suffer fools gladly—" Askell appeared to realise how that sounded, in relation to himself, and shifted again in his seat. "We quite often disagreed on the best way forward, but we always worked it out. We could respect each other's point of view."

"I see."

"He was very driven. Work was almost everything to him. It wasn't so much the money; it was almost as if he constantly had to prove himself. I don't know why that was, I never asked him."

"You didn't have that kind of relationship?"

Askell blinked. "No. Like I said, we weren't close. We had a strong and respectful working relationship but we weren't – weren't emotionally close, I suppose you'd say."

Kate broke in, knowing that Olbeck wouldn't mind. "Would you say he was emotionally close to anyone else? Anyone who works here, perhaps?"

Askell looked uncomfortable. "Well, I – I'm not sure."

Kate glanced at Olbeck. "Would you say Simon Farraday was happily married?"

Askell did more than blink at that question. He reared his head back, as if Kate had shouted in his face. "Oh, my word, miss – I'm sorry, Sergeant – I – I suppose so. They seemed happy enough to me."

Kate wasn't sure whether he was being deliberately vague or whether he was just the kind of man made extremely uncomfortable at the thought of having to talk about emotions. She suspected the latter, given his earlier answers. "Do you know his wife, Mia Farraday, well?"

Askell seemed to have recovered his composure a little. "Mia? No, not very well. I like her, she seems like a nice woman. A good mother, always there for her children. Very devoted. Of course, Simon had very long working hours, so it was good that at least one of their parents was on hand."

Kate nodded and scribbled a meaningless doodle on her pad, away from Ewan Askell's eyes. She saw him look nervously at her pen. "So, you didn't know her well? Did she come here to the office very often?"

"No, not very often. Not much more than every few months, I suppose. She didn't really have a lot to do with the business, although, of course, she is a minority shareholder."

That was something they would have to take a look at, thought Kate – Simon Farraday's business. In fact, they'd have to take an in depth look at a lot of things – the board of directors, the clients, the financials. She stifled a yawn at the thought. Business really didn't interest her in the slightest.

Olbeck asked Askell about the last time he had seen Simon Farraday, the day before his murder. As Kate scribbled down her notes, she listened with half an ear. Farraday had apparently been quite normal – 'chipper' was Ewan Askell's word – and had mentioned he was planning to play a round of golf at the local course at the weekend. Askell said that he himself had hoped to get in a round or two if the weather had held.

"Do you play together?" asked Kate.

Askell looked a touch embarrassed. "No, no, not as such. But we do tend to run into each other at the club, because we're both members."

Kate got the particulars of the golf club. She recognised the name – it was the most expensive and exclusive of the local courses. *That figures*. Something else to check out and, with an inner sigh, she added it to her list.

*

"So, what did you think of Mr Askell?" Olbeck asked as they drove away forty minutes later. They had quickly checked Farraday's office, and found nothing of suspicion or interest, and had a quick interview with his personal assistant, Claire Young, a twenty-something blonde with the slight tinge of an Australian accent. She'd been the only other person to have shown visible signs of grief for Simon Farraday, apart from his wife. At one point in the interview she'd broken down in tears. Kate and Olbeck had ascertained her movements on the night of the murder – Claire had been out with a large group of her girlfriends – and taken her contact details.

"Askell? Not sure." Kate read through her list of notes once more, in short snatches, as reading too much in a moving car made her feel sick. "Not sure. *Really* not sure, actually. He seems – evasive. Or at least uncomfortable with answering questions about – well, anything to do with Simon Farraday."

"Yes, I know what you mean." Olbeck glanced at the sat nav screen, checking the route back to Abbeyford. "There's something, isn't there... Do you get the impression that he and Farraday weren't exactly on great terms?"

"Yes, definitely."

"Hmm." Olbeck pursed his lips. "Well, he's staying on the suspect list for now, at least. Although we don't have a shred of evidence and he's got an alibi—"

"Oh, he has, has he? I was going to ask about that."

"Oh yes. He was at some local history society meeting that night and gave one of his fellow historians a lift home and didn't get back to his own place until well after midnight. So, it's *unlikely* he was involved, but..."

Kate knew what he meant. "Yes, I know. Remember Jack Dorsey and Alexander Hargreaves? That whole set up there reminded me a bit of that."

"Yes, I agree. Now—" Olbeck glanced over at her. "What do you think about calling into Farraday's golf club? It's on the way home, and we could see if anyone can tell us anything useful?"

"Concurred, Captain."

Olbeck said nothing but he grinned as he accelerated away down the road.

Chapter Six

IT WAS RAINING HEAVILY BY the time Kate and Olbeck got back to the office in the late afternoon. Kate shrugged off her wet coat and hung it over the radiator, which some enterprising soul had turned on and up to full heat. She collapsed in her chair, feeling as if she'd been gone for four days, rather than a matter of hours, especially when she opened her mail box and groaned at the long line of unanswered emails. She and Olbeck had grabbed a quick sandwich on the way back from the golf course but that seemed an inadequate lunch. She'd stock up on some vending machine crisps, and when she got home, she'd order the biggest pizza it was possible to buy. *And* extra garlic bread.

"Bird. Where've you been all day?"

Kate looked up at Chloe, who was standing by her desk and munching on a chocolate bar. Her stomach growled. "Out interviewing Simon Farraday's work mates and golfing buddies."

"Get anything?"

"A few possibilities. Nothing earth-shattering, though."

"Oh well. Theo's found something interesting on the CCTV from the square."

Tiredness and hunger were forgotten for a moment. Kate sat up a little. "Oh, yes?"

"Yes. Come and see." Chloe obviously caught sight of Kate staring hungrily at the remainder of her chocolate. "Want a bit?"

"Yes, please."

They gathered around Theo's desk while he found the appropriate file on his computer, dropping crumbs of chocolate on his keyboard as they finished their snack.

"Oy, women. Stop." Theo turned his keyboard upside down and shook it. A quantity of fluff, crumbs and other assorted detritus fell out.

"Ugh," said Chloe. "You know that there are more germs on a keyboard than there are on the average toilet?"

"There are with you two around." Brushing the fluff and dust onto the floor, Theo turned back to his computer. "Now, look here." His slim, brown finger traced the flickering progress of a dark figure on the footage playing on his computer screen.

"Picture quality's crap." Chloe leaned in to get a better view.

"Yeah, I know, but it was a rainy night, the camera there is old and it's the best I've got, okay?" They all craned to look. There on screen, a small dark figure walked around the edge of Market Square. It was almost impossible to make out anything of detail, due to the grainy footage, but it was just possible to see that the figure was wearing some kind of dark, hooded coat and was wearing high-heeled shoes.

"A woman," said Kate.

Theo threw her a look. "Well, I suppose it could be a very small transvestite, but yes, I'd hazard a guess that it's a woman. Now look..."

They all watched as the figure opened the door of the Farraday's town house and went inside.

"Are they using a key?" Kate asked, squinting to try and make it out. It was a useless task – the footage was just too unclear. She looked at the time clock on the piece of digital film. It was nine fifty-three pm when the woman – or whoever – let herself in, whether by key or by an unlocked door. "Is that it?" she asked.

"Pretty much."

Kate frowned. "We don't see her leave?"

Both Chloe and Theo turned to look at her with the air of people saving the best for last. "No," said Chloe, folding her arms across her chest. "We don't."

Kate's frown deepened. "What? Not at all?"

"No." Chloe smiled rather grimly.

"That's—" Kate broke off for a moment, looking back at the black and white flicker of Theo's computer screen. "Come on, that's not possible. She must have gone out the back way. *Is* there a back way?"

"Yes." Theo was looking like someone in possession of a juicy secret he was desperate to impart. "But the footage covering that street doesn't have anything on it either."

Kate stared at them both. "*Nothing*? For the whole night? Right up until Mia Farraday arrives in the morning?"

Theo shook his head. "Nada. Not a dickie bird."

Kate scoffed. "Oh, come on. That's our murderer, most probably, and they just vanish into thin air? Have you told Anderton that?"

Both Theo and Chloe looked a little sheepish. "No," said Theo after a moment.

"Right. Because it's not possible." Kate looked back at the screen, rubbing her fingers along her jaw. "There must be a missing piece of footage, or something."

Theo looked even more sheepish. "Well..."

Kate looked up sharply. "What?"

"Well, there *is* about a fifteen-minute interval when the tape goes on the fritz. The camera in the square. About two am in the morning. Only fifteen minutes or so."

Kate rolled her eyes and sagged. "Well, that's it then, isn't it? That's when she left. God knows how she timed it right, or maybe it's just our bad luck and coincidence—"

"Maybe," said Chloe. She sounded uneasy. "I don't know, though."

"Oh, come *on*. Fifteen minute of no footage, well after the murder's been committed, where there's no tape evidence of anyone coming or going? The defence team would be on that like – like a rocket."

Chloe shrugged. "Well, if there's no footage of anyone else entering or leaving the house in all that other time, and the only time we don't have covered is after the murder is committed, then that woman – or whoever she is – seen entering the house at nine fifty-three is the murderer. Got to be."

Kate looked at the screen again. "Not necessarily."

"Well, then – what do you mean?"

Kate tapped Theo on the shoulder. "Theo, how far back in these tapes have you looked?"

"What?"

"I mean, have you just looked at footage from the night of the murder?"

Theo looked confused. "Yeah. So far – I haven't had time to do anything else."

"What are you getting at, Kate?" asked Chloe.

Kate raised both hands in a shrugging gesture. "It's just an idea but what if the murderer actually entered the house before the day of the murder?"

There was a short silence. "What, and just – stayed there?" asked Theo.

"Perhaps. It's only an idea."

As one, they all looked at the screen again. Theo had paused the footage at the clip of the dark figure letting themselves in at the door.

"Well, I suppose it's possible," said Chloe, slowly.

"So, who's that, then?" Theo demanded, pointing

at the figure on the screen. They all regarded it again, as if the answer would suddenly reveal itself.

"It wouldn't—" Kate began, and then shook her head and shut up.

"What?"

"It wouldn't be – Simon Farraday, would it?" she said, waiting for Theo's laughter at the thought. It didn't come. They all three leaned closer to the screen to see if they could work it out.

"I don't think so," Chloe pronounced, a few moments later. "Whoever it is, he or she is quite small. Farraday was a good six foot. And this person has small feet – he didn't."

"Mm." Kate blew out her cheeks in frustration. "Well. Like I said, it was only an idea."

Unnoticed by any of them, Olbeck had wandered up to see what they were doing. His sudden question made them all jump. "What's all this?"

Kate explained as quickly and as simply as she could. Olbeck listened, nodding. "Well, I think the quickest thing to do is interview Mia Farraday again, see if she knows if anyone's been in the house in the last week or so."

"I'll start going through the earlier footage," promised Theo. "First thing tomorrow."

That made Kate look at the clock. Time had raced by while they were working and it was almost seven o'clock. Merlin would be yowling for his dinner.

"I'll call for you first thing," said Olbeck, as they

all said their goodbyes and prepared to leave the office. "We'll interview Mia Farraday together. I'm sure there's a lot more she can tell us."

"I'm sure, too." Kate clapped him on the shoulder in a farewell gesture and then went to gather her bag and coat, yawning and thinking with longing of her home, and her cat, and a very large pizza.

Chapter Seven

WHEN OLBECK DROVE INTO THE driveway of the Farraday residence the next morning, the only car to be seen on the wide concrete sweep of the driveway was a battered looking little Fiat. Kate gave it a puzzled glance as their own car parked alongside it. Surely that wasn't Mia Farraday's car? Women like her (in her own mind, Kate was feeling a little guilty for pigeonholing the woman like this, but she knew what she was trying to say) – women like Mia, stay at home mothers partnered to wealthy men, usually drove gigantic gleaming four wheel drives or something smaller but fashionable, like a new Mini or a Beetle.

The little mystery was solved as the door was answered by Mandy, one of the victim liaison officers. Kate and Olbeck knew her quite well and they exchanged greetings tempered in enthusiasm by the sombreness of their surroundings.

"I'm only here for today," Mandy whispered as they made their way down the corridor to the huge living area at the back of the house. Mia Farraday was seated at the dining table, concentrating on the screen of a small silver laptop. The sight of it made Kate recall that Simon Farraday's work and home laptops and computer equipment were currently being examined by the IT department back at the station. She made a mental note to check with Sam Hollingsworth, the head of the IT, whether they'd found anything interesting yet. Presumably Mia's laptop would have also been seized, especially when she'd been considered a suspect. Clearly, IT had found nothing of interest on it and had returned it to its owner.

As if Mia had read her mind, she looked up and caught Kate's eye. "Good morning, DS Redman." Kate saw her looking quizzically at Olbeck, who apparently she hadn't met. Kate hastened to introduce him.

Mandy excused herself and walked over to the kitchen area, so she was still in view but more or less out of earshot.

"How are you, Mrs Farraday?" asked Kate.

Mia smiled wanly. She looked better than she had at their previous meeting – the cut on her lip was healing – but she looked as though she was losing weight. The sharp angle of her cheekbones was so acute it looked painfully as though the bone was about to protrude through the skin of her cheeks. "I'm surviving. I can't really say I'm doing anything better than that."

For the first time, it occurred to Kate to wonder where the Farraday children were. She recollected that there were three of them. Perhaps at school? She asked as much.

"James is. He's nine. Milo is at pre-school and Sarah's taken Tilly out to her playgroup."

Of course, Sarah was the nanny. That was somebody else it might be worth talking to. Kate asked how the children were coping and regretted it when Mia's face crumpled.

"They're doing as well as can be expected," she said in a colourless voice. Another white handkerchief was extracted from the pocket of her jeans to wipe her eyes. "Luckily Tilly's too little to really understand. Well, so is Milo, I suppose. It's James that's—" She broke off, her voice wobbling, and turned away for a moment.

When she turned back, she had a smile on her face but one that looked as though it was actually causing her physical pain. "I'm so sorry, I haven't even asked if you wanted coffee, or something."

"I can make that," called Mandy, from the kitchen.

"I like having her here," Mia whispered, stowing the damp handkerchief back in her pocket. "It's another pair of hands to help and it just seems – oh, a little less lonely with someone else here."

"Do you not have any relatives or friends that might be able to come and help you out?" Kate asked sympathetically.

Mia shook her head. "My brother lives overseas, and my friends are all so busy, I couldn't impose on them..." She trailed off for a second. "There's nothing *wrong* with me, you know, it's just – it's just grief. And shock. And I've got Sarah, I suppose."

She broke off abruptly, staring out of the enormous expanse of glass at the back of the room. Mandy brought over some mugs of coffee and a plate of biscuits.

Olbeck and Kate settled themselves around the dining table. Mia sat back down in her chair and flipped the lid of her laptop closed. "Your lot just returned that this morning," she said, a hint of irritation in her voice. "I'm just trying to catch up with everything I've missed over the last week."

Olbeck obviously recognised that as a good place to jump in. "Are you very involved in your husband's business, Mrs Farraday?"

Mia looked surprised. "With Porthos? No, not at all. I'm a shareholder but that's it. I don't have anything to do with the day to day running of the business." She glanced down at her closed laptop and added "No, it's more the property side of things that I have to worry about. The holiday let and the, well, the day to day running of the house. That was what I was talking about."

Talking about her role in the family seemed to bring her some comfort and a little colour came back into her hollowed cheeks. Kate found herself wondering whether Simon Farraday had left a will.

Surely he must have done, a man as wealthy as he had been?

"We met your husband's business partner yesterday. Well, his deputy, I suppose. Ewan Askell." Olbeck said this rather apropos of nothing, but Kate recognised his attempt to gain a little bit more information on the man.

Mia half smiled. "Oh, Ewan? Yes, he came round yesterday with some flowers. Very kind of him. He *is* kind, though."

"You know him well?"

"No. Only through Simon." Mia was silent for a moment and then added "Simon never had much time for Ewan. He dismissed him as a bit of a fool. But then he was like that with anyone who wasn't much like him."

"Really?"

Mia half smiled. "Simon was a very intelligent man. *Very* intelligent. And that sometimes made him quite – quite impatient with anyone who he thought couldn't keep up with him, intellectually."

Kate regarded Simon Farraday's wife for a moment. She would have said that Mia Farraday, given her articulacy and her manner, was an intelligent woman. Had his wife been one of the people to whom Simon Farraday had shown his impatience? Did she miss him or mourn him? Kate would have said, by the reaction she'd got from Mia on their first meeting, that it went without saying. Now, she wondered a little. Mia wouldn't have been the first wife who, while their husbands were alive, had gone through married life wrapped in a happy bubble of denial. Once death came, that bubble as often as not popped and reality was laid bare.

"How did you and Simon meet, Mrs Farraday?" she asked, curious now to get some more background on the Farradays' marriage.

Mia gave her a surprised glance, as if she'd forgotten Kate was in the room. "I was an intern at his first company. It was my first placement after university." She smiled rather ruefully. "My parents weren't best thrilled, me dating a man fifteen years older than myself, and the boss of the company at that time. Still..." She made an eloquent shrugging gesture. "There we go."

"Where did you go to university?" asked Kate, just for form's sake. She was confirmed in her view of Mia Farraday being at least of average intelligence, given that she'd gained a place on a degree course.

"Edinburgh. I did History." Mia looked at her closed laptop. "Gosh, that seems such a long time ago now."

They were interrupted by the sight of a young woman striding along in front of the glass doors, with a toddler settled on her hip. She was tall and slender, with thick blonde hair pulled back into a messy bun. They all watched her in silence as she opened the back door with her free hand and came into the room.

"Oh! Sorry," said the woman, looking a little startled at the sight of them all. Clearly the sunlight shining on the glass outside hadn't allowed her to see through it while she was walking past. The toddler, a beautiful little girl with dark, shiny curls, looked at them silently and put her thumb in her mouth.

"This is Sarah Collins, our nanny," said Mia. Her tone was neutral, and that in itself made Kate glance at her. What was the relationship between the two women? Warm and friendly or cool and professional? Or antagonistic?

Sarah smiled around at them all rather nervously as Mia introduced the two police officers.

"Good morning, Ms Collins," said Olbeck with a friendly smile. "We'd like to have a quick word with you at some point, if that's okay with you – and with Mrs Farraday?"

Mia nodded. "That's fine with me." She held out her arms to the toddler. "Hello, Tillikins! How's my girl?"

Kate watched as Sarah relinquished the little girl. Tilly went to her mother happily and with a smile on her face, her little thumb popping out of her mouth as she flung her arms around her mother's neck. She wondered what Simon's relationship with his children had been like. From the sounds of it, he'd been buried in work most of the time. Work and extra-marital relations? She found herself suddenly feeling sorry for Mia Farraday, who, whether or not she'd known about her husband's infidelity (and had there just been the one, the one who might have killed him, or many?) had obviously been left to shoulder the majority of the domestic chores. Even if she did have a nanny.

"I'll be in my room," Sarah said, looking to Mia as if for approval. Mia nodded again, without looking at her, her attention on Tilly.

Kate and Olbeck exchanged a glance. It was going to be a little tricky to question Mia about some of her husband's more questionable activities if a two-year-old child was going to be present.

Mia seemed, without mentioning it, to understand this. "Come on, Tilly, let's see if we can find you some Peppa Pig to watch while I talk to these grown-ups."

"Peppa!" said Tilly with enthusiasm.

"Yes, Peppa. Come on, let's get you settled over here."

Kate and Olbeck waited while the big television was turned on and a nest of cushions made for Tilly in front of it. When her daughter was settled with a sippy cup of juice, Mia came back and sat down at the table. She looked tired.

"I'm sorry, I know you've got things you need to ask me." She slumped a little in her seat before pushing herself back upright. "Fire away."

Olbeck cleared his throat. "Were you aware that your husband—" He stopped for a minute and changed tack. "I'm sorry, but was your husband faithful to you,

Mrs Farraday?" He added quickly, "I know it must be painful, I'm sorry."

Mia didn't look angry but something tightened in her face. "I didn't *know*—" She broke off, pinching the bridge of her narrow nose. "I suppose I had an inkling. I didn't ever ask him about it. To be honest—" She broke off again, looking a little shamefaced. "To be honest, I didn't *want* to know. Cowardly of me, I know, but – but even if he was cheating on me, what was I going to do about it? I've got three young children, I don't work, I haven't got an income of my own. And Simon and I, we were fine together. Most of the time. I mean, we had our ups and downs, all couples do but there was nothing..." She fell silent again. "I just didn't want to know. If there was anything. I certainly didn't realise he was into all of – all of *that*."

Olbeck spoke cautiously. "By that, you mean the—"

Now Mia did look angry. "Do you want me to spell it out? *That*, the handcuffs, the leather. I had no idea—" She broke off, folding her lips together as if to keep her anger in.

She meant it, Kate realised. She hadn't had any idea. No wonder she'd reacted like she had on finding him. Not just the shock of his death but the manner of it. Again, she felt a brief but keen stab of sympathy for the woman.

"I understand, Mrs Farraday." When Olbeck wanted to be soothing, he could be very soothing indeed. "So you had no idea who he might have been meeting that night at the townhouse?"

"No. I haven't any idea at all."

"You haven't received any messages from anyone? Anything odd at all?"

"No."

"You – forgive me – you never checked your husband's phone or computer, or anything like that?"

"No," Mia said, stonily. "I told you I didn't want to know if anything was going on."

Olbeck sat back in his chair. Kate took this as her cue to sit forward. "Mrs Farraday, you've mentioned that you had an inkling recently that something was going on. Had there ever been any incidents in the past that made you – uneasy, perhaps?"

Mia stared at her. "I don't understand what you mean, sorry."

"I mean, had Simon ever had an affair in the past or – or a flirtation, or anything like that?"

Mia stared at her for a moment longer, before dropping her gaze. "No. I don't think so. If he had, I didn't know about it."

I get it, Kate thought to herself silently. *You didn't want to know.*

A short silence fell. Kate could hear Mandy clattering about unobtrusively in the kitchen and a series of oinks coming from the television. Tilly giggled, a high, sweet innocent laugh. Mia's face crumpled briefly at the sound.

"Mrs Farraday, it would really help us if you could give us a list of anyone who might have been in the townhouse over the past few weeks. Say, over the last fortnight." Kate glanced down at her notes, checking what she'd scribbled down yesterday. "Just so we can eliminate them from our enquiries."

Mia turned back to face her from where she had been watching her daughter. "People in the townhouse? Oh, it hasn't been rented out for a while, I know that. Not for at least a month. That's why we were using it as an office, to be honest, it was a bit of extra space."

"So you haven't had any guests in there recently?"

"No. I'll double check the booking forms, just to be sure, but I know from memory that we haven't."

Kate nodded. "What about anyone else? Any friends that might have gone there? Any maintenance workers or cleaners, perhaps?"

Mia looked doubtful. "Our cleaners would have been there." She gave Kate their names. "But I don't think anyone else has, apart from me and Simon." Her face contracted again briefly. "And whoever he was with that – that night."

There was another short silence. Kate looked over at Olbeck, signalling with her eyes.

"Well, that's all we need to know for now, Mrs Farraday," said Olbeck. He returned Kate's glance and they both got to their feet. "We'd like to have a quick word with Ms Collins now, if that's okay with you?"

"That's fine," said Mia, dully. She was staring at the back of her daughter's dark, curly head.

"I'm sorry to have had to ask you these questions but it's essential for the investigation."

Mia gave him a ghost of a smile, unexpectedly painful to see. "That's all right," she said, almost in a whisper. Then she got up and went and sat with Tilly, curled up with her daughter in the nest of cushions, watching the antics of the animated pink pigs on the screen in front of them.

Chapter Eight

KATE EXPECTED TO FIND SARAH Collins in a typical young woman's bedroom; posters on the walls, mess on the floor. As it turned out, the Farraday nanny had an entire suite of rooms to herself: bedroom, bathroom, galley kitchen and living room, and it was very neat and clean. Sarah herself was curled on the green-checked sofa in the living room, tapping and swiping busily at her phone. Kate was relieved to see she was a normal millennial in that respect.

Her respect for the girl increased when Sarah quickly put away the phone and sat up expectantly as she and Olbeck came into the room.

"Nice place you've got here," said Kate, sitting down on the opposite sofa.

Sarah smiled. "It's great, actually. My last place, I was up in the attic which had barely been converted. It was freezing in winter. This is much better."

"It's a good job, then?"

"Oh yes." The enthusiasm in the girl's voice didn't

sound faked. "The kids are lovely and, like you can see, I have a great living space."

"What hours do you work?"

"Eight 'til eight, normally, although obviously I'm not always on duty. Like now. If I've only got Tilly to look after, as likely as not Mrs Farraday will take her and I get a bit of time free."

"Are you often here at night or do you get some nights off?"

Sarah shrugged. "It depends. Mia – Mrs Farraday – she has quite a lot of hobbies, you know, like Pilates, and she goes to the gym a lot and stuff. So she's out two or three times a week, so obviously I have to be here then. But otherwise, I'm free."

"How long have you worked for the Farradays?"

Sarah pushed a strand of hair back from her face. She seemed unfazed by the question. "Just over a year. I think they had au pairs before but then Mia's mum got ill – well, she *was* ill anyway, she had Alzheimer's – but she got quite a lot worse and Mia couldn't cope. So they had to have someone a bit more full time."

Kate scribbled that down. "Yes, I see. Quite distressing for Mrs Farraday, I'd imagine. Is her mother any worse?"

Sarah's face clouded. "Oh – she died. About five months ago. Mia was obviously – well, she was really broken up by it, and so they kept me on to give her a hand." She smiled again and looked slightly smug. "She relies on me, now."

"Do you and Mrs Farraday get on well?"

Sarah's bright smile dimmed a little. "Oh, yes. We get on fine."

Kate paused before asking her next question. There was something just a little – guarded – in Sarah's response. "What about Mr Farraday, Simon Farraday?"

The smile had gone completely now. "What do you mean?"

Kate smiled. "Well, did you get on well?"

She saw Sarah relax a little. "Oh, well, yeah. We got on fine when I actually saw him. He was hardly ever here, though."

Just as Kate had suspected. She nodded and let Olbeck take over, listening to him asking Sarah about her previous experience, and what she had been doing in the crucial hours of the evening of Simon Farraday's murder. Her gaze roamed the living room, which was tastefully but neutrally decorated, much as the Farradays' townhouse had been. Not much evidence of Sarah Collins' personality appeared, which was slightly odd, given that she'd worked for the Farradays for over a year.

Nothing that Sarah mentioned gave Kate particular pause. She confirmed that Mia had gone out to visit her friend, Dorothy Smelton, on the night of the murder, but she wasn't able to confirm when she'd arrived back as she'd been asleep. Not that it really mattered, given Mia's alibi was already firmly established. Kate was unsurprised to hear that Mia obviously filled her time as best she could, with exercise and hobbies and visits to friends. The components of someone making the best of a lonely marriage.

*

"So, what do you think?" Kate asked Olbeck, as they drove away from the Farradays' residence, along the winding driveway. Even more bluebells had appeared in the woodlands, great shimmering masses of them in azure drifts, enough to take your breath away. "Wow, look at that."

"Very nice," said Olbeck. "Be a good place for a picnic, hey? Pity it's private. Anyway, what were you saying?"

"Just asking what you think about the domestic arrangements at *chez* Farraday."

"Oh, that." It wasn't very easy to shrug whilst driving a car, but Olbeck somehow managed it. "Well, I think there's something the nanny's not telling us."

"Me too." Kate smiled to herself, pleased they had both picked up on Sarah Collins' slight change of manner.

"It's probably nothing sinister, though. You know what it's like being a – well, not a *servant*, exactly. Subservient, perhaps. You might have a little something on your employers that they might not like you knowing."

"Mmm." Kate watched the last of the bluebells disappear from view with regret. "Do you get the impression that Simon Farraday was a bit of an arsehole?"

Olbeck grinned. "That's your professional opinion, is it?"

"Yep."

"Well, yes, actually. He sounds like a right, arrogant piece of work. But that's not necessarily why he was killed."

"No, true." Kate glanced at the dashboard clock. "I wonder if Sam's got anywhere with his computer yet?"

"We'll soon see."

*

WHEN THEY ARRIVED BACK AT the station, both Kate and Olbeck immediately headed down to the basement, where the IT department was located. Sam Hollingsworth was in a meeting in his office with the door closed, but one of his minions, a wiry young man called Josh with an enormous Afro and thick, black-framed glasses, obligingly went and fetched the laptop and powered it up at Sam's empty desk, so Kate and Olbeck could see the results of the investigation for themselves.

"So, anything pertinent?" asked Olbeck, leaning forward to see.

"Oh yeah, yeah. First thing we noticed, it's stuffed with porn, right? Nothing dodgy though. Well—" Josh appeared to reconsider. "Nothing *really* dodgy,

I mean. No kids or animals. But plenty of kink. Bondage, sub-dom, stuff like that."

"Right." Kate exchanged a glance with Olbeck. "That sounds par for the course. Anything else?"

Josh grew serious. "Yeah. He was a member of a hook-up site, you know, for people who want to meet up for sex. Stuff like that."

"Right. Let's have a look."

Kate and Olbeck crowded around Josh, who sat down and began bringing up various screens with practised ease. A website with branding familiar to Kate came up.

"Oh, I know this one," she exclaimed and immediately realised where she'd gone wrong. Both Josh and Olbeck were grinning. "Not because I'm *on* it, you idiots. I've seen it before, with the Valentine case. You know, Mark. The pig hearts." Josh looked mystified and somewhat alarmed. "It must have been before you started," said Kate. "Anyway, it's not important. But this site—" She gestured at the screen. The moody blues and greens of the website highlighted the gold lettering of the logo *4Adults*. "It's a site for people looking for sex, basically. No strings attached."

"Yeah, like I said." Josh's fingers moved over the keyboard in a blur. "He joined about six months ago. You can see from his private messages that he's arranged to meet at least—" He quickly counted under his breath. "At least six women since he's been on the site."

Olbeck whistled. "He has, has he? How do you know they're women?"

"Well, I don't, not for definite. But most people have it on their avatar, either a pink or blue star." He gestured with his finger.

Kate grunted. "How original."

"There's no way of knowing that they're *actually* women, though. Anyone can be anything behind a computer screen."

Kate peered closer. "I don't suppose anyone's using their real names, either?"

Josh barked a laugh. "No."

"Right." Kate straightened up.

"Josh, this is great, thank you," said Olbeck. "We'll need to trace everyone Simon Farraday has contacted through this website. I suppose we won't know until we interview them whether he *actually* met them or just wanted to."

"Yeah, s'pose so." Josh eased his shoulders and began to click his fingers on the keyboard again.

"Wait," said Kate, suddenly curious. "Is there anything in his messages about meeting up on the night of the murder?"

Josh gave her a quizzical look. "Yeah, of course. That's the first thing I checked. I printed it out." He fished around on Sam's desk and found the piece of paper he was looking for. "Here you go."

Kate and Olbeck bent to read it in silence.

Maxpower: can't wait to see you tonight. Everything's ready.

Mermaid68: can't wait. I'll be there as soon as I can get away.

Kate looked up with a curled lip. "'*Maxpower*'? That's Simon Farraday's user name?"

Josh was grinning. "Yeah, that's him."

Kate shook her head. "What a *tool*."

"Fancies himself, doesn't he?"

"He *did*," said Olbeck briefly, and that recalled the other two to the gravity of what they were doing. Kate bent back to read in silence.

Maxpower: You know where to come?

Mermaid68: I hope so! ;)

Maxpower: LOL. You bet. You know I meant the address ;)

Mermaid68: No problem. Will you leave me a key?

Maxpower: Will leave the door unlocked. Won't be able to let you in as you know I'll be a bit tied up ;) ;)

Mermaid68: That's the plan ;)

Maxpower: Text me when you're on your way and I'll get ready. CU later sexy xx

*

THAT WAS THE END OF the transcript. Kate and Olbeck straightened up at the same time. Kate fought not to let her grimace show on her face. She felt a nauseous mixture of repugnance, horror and, worst of all, pity. The way Simon Farraday used teenage text speak whilst still bothering to punctuate correctly made her want to bite her fist in sympathetic embarrassment.

"Poor bloke," said Olbeck, clearly feeling much the same.

Josh was obviously too young and too inexperienced to be thus affected. He made a face and said "Yeah, well, obviously I went back through the whole of his messages tracing this mermaid sixty-eight."

Young and naïve he might be, but Josh was clearly good at his job. "You did?" Kate asked with gratitude.

"Yeah. Got everything here. Sounds like he met her, well, *met* her as in online, about six months ago. There's messages going back that far. You can see for yourself."

Josh handed over a plastic folder containing the print outs of the messages. There were enough in the folder to justify taking it away and studying it at leisure. Kate glanced at Olbeck. "That's my job for the afternoon."

"Good stuff." The two of them prepared to leave. "Thanks, Josh. Good work. Could you tell Sam we might need to see him as well, later on?"

"Sure."

Kate paused on her way out of the cubicle. "Josh, we really need to trace whoever this mermaid sixty-eight is. I assume you're on that now?"

Josh pointed his fingers at her in a gun shape. "I am *on* it."

Kate grinned. "Good to know. We'll need all of

them, all the people that Simon Farraday contacted and met, but she – if it is a she – is top priority. Okay?"

"Okay, boss."

*

THE TWO OF THEM CLIMBED back up the stairs to light and space. As they passed the double doors that led to the main reception area of the station, Kate could see the sunlight through the glass panels of the inner and outer doors. Another lovely day, and she'd be stuck reading through computer transcripts in a stuffy office...

"Mind if I take these off site?" she asked Olbeck on impulse.

He looked surprised. "No. Just sign them out, as normal."

"Thanks," said Kate gratefully.

She headed back to the office to complete the paperwork and pick up her bag and coat (it may have been a lovely day but Kate was too experienced with the vagaries of the English climate to trust it this early in the Spring). Chloe was sitting at her desk, frowning at her computer screen. Saying goodbye to her, Kate realised she was due at Andrew Stanton's for dinner that evening and that she still hadn't arranged for someone to accompany her. Not that she should mind going on her own but... Why hadn't she thought of Chloe? She asked her now.

"Sorry it's late notice but I forgot about it, to be honest."

Chloe looked pleased to be asked. "That's all right. Sure, I'll come." She grinned and said "It's the closest thing I've come to a hot date for a while, I can tell you."

Kate laughed. "Good. He's nice, actually, Andrew. I haven't met the wife but she'll probably be all right."

"Well, it'll mean a drink at least."

"Some good ones. Andrew's a bit of a wine buff."

"Great. I'm sold."

Kate pulled on her jacket. "Come round to mine beforehand, and we'll go together. I don't mind driving."

"Thanks. See you later. Bird."

"Bird," said Kate, laughing again. Then, flapping a hand in farewell, and feeling a bit more comfortable about the evening's appointment, she left the office.

Chapter Nine

MRS STANTON, WHOSE NAME WAS Juliet, turned out to be as nice as Kate had hoped she would be. She was much more round and comfortable looking than Kate had imagined, although as Hamish Stanton was only ten months old, it probably was not that surprising. In physical type, she was very different to Kate, with ash-blonde hair, soft features and dressed in what Kate recognised as top-to-toe Boden designs. Kate, who considered that she'd dressed slightly more fancily than she would normally have, felt positively over-dressed in her black velvet jacket and gauzy blouse.

Chloe was wearing a black suit as normal. Kate had never seen her wear anything else. She wondered briefly, as they shook hands with the Stantons in the hallway of their house and handed over their bottles of wine, whether Chloe had pyjamas made in a similar shade and style, just in a slightly softer material.

Andrew had reacted to Chloe's presence with an unmistakable look of surprise, which, good-mannered man that he was, was quickly suppressed. Kate had introduced Chloe as her 'friend and workmate' and she had a momentary impish thought as to whether she should play up the 'this is actually my lesbian partner' angle for a laugh. A second later, she dismissed the idea. This evening was going to be awkward enough as it was.

The first half hour, as drinks were poured and chairs were offered, and Juliet darted back and forth to the kitchen to check on the food, threatened to be just as sticky as Kate had been worriedly anticipating. Luckily, Stanton Junior, or Hamish James, as he was more commonly known, proved to be such a draw in his adorable blue and white sleepsuit, appliqued with little white mice, that any awkwardness was immediately smoothed over. There was almost a tussle between Kate and Chloe as to who got the first cuddle.

"He's absolutely gorgeous," Kate exclaimed to Andrew and was rewarded by his pleased and proud smile. For a second, she felt a pang of something that was dangerously near regret. She knew that, if she'd wanted it, Andrew would have married her. Hamish could have been hers. She kept her head bent down over Hamish's downy head for a moment, struggling to process how she was feeling. Sanity soon returned. She'd broken up with Andrew because she hadn't loved him. That would have been a disastrous basis for a marriage and, deep down, she knew it. No regrets, she told herself sternly.

She looked up, smiling brightly. Chloe was

looking at her rather keenly, and for a moment, Kate wondered uncomfortably if the other woman had read her mind. She was a good cop, after all, used to seeing what other people were trying to hide.

"About time for your bed, young man." Andrew was holding his arms out for his son. Kate relinquished his soft little body reluctantly, and she and Chloe waved 'bye-bye' to him as he was carried from the room.

The food was good but quite plain and unpretentious. That surprised Kate, given her memories of the fine dining she used to enjoy whilst going out with Andrew. But then, looking at the comfortable mess lying around his house, the house she remembered as once painfully neat and ordered, she had to admit that he'd changed. She thought of her own house, also neat and ordered, and just the way she wanted it. Could she change too? *Should* she? Did she even want to?

It was an effort not to fall silent with all the emotional examination she was subjecting herself to. She made an effort to join in the conversation, which was actually quite interesting. Andrew and Juliet had met out in Sierra Leone, when they were both working for *Médecins Sans Frontières*, the medical charity, and they were sharing their reminiscences of the different parts of Africa where they'd worked and travelled. It turned out that Chloe had been to several of the places they'd mentioned and the three of them were getting along like a house on fire. Having never so much as set foot on the continent, Kate was unable to contribute much, but she made herself nod enthusiastically at points in the conversation where she felt it was demanded.

All in all, the evening passed a great deal more pleasantly than Kate had anticipated. Having Chloe there helped – when Chloe Wapping wanted to be sociable, she could be very sociable – but Kate was also conscious of the fact that she'd faced up to a situation that she could and would have avoided if it had been up to her. That always made you feel better about yourself, she thought, as they said their goodbyes at the end of the evening.

"You're welcome to leave your car at my place if you want," she told Chloe as she drove them home.

"Thanks, Kate, but I'm fine to drive. I only had a few glasses early on."

"No problem, then." They'd reached Kate's house by this point and Kate concentrated on reversing into the space outside her house, always a bit tricky. "Do you fancy a cup of tea or something before you go?"

Chloe considered and then glanced at her watch. "All right, then. It's not the witching hour just yet. Why not?"

Merlin twined around Kate's ankles as she made the tea. It was far too late to make up a fire in the living room – it had been so warm for the past few days that Kate hadn't even bothered to bring in more firewood – but it was a little chilly to be sitting around, so Kate flipped the switch for the central heating and listened with satisfaction as the boiler roared to life.

The two women flopped onto opposite sofas and reached for their mugs of tea.

"Thanks for inviting me," said Chloe. "They're nice, aren't they?"

"They are," Kate admitted. "I was worried it was going to be a bit awkward but—"

"Why?"

"Oh, you know. An ex-boyfriend and all that."

"But that's ancient history, isn't it? You surely don't still fancy him?"

"No!" said Kate, shocked. "It's not that—"

"Yeah, I know. But as it turned out, it was fine, right?"

"Right."

They sipped their tea in silence for a moment. Kate saw Chloe's gaze go to a photograph on the mantelpiece, one of a smartly dressed Kate and Tin with their arms around one another, grinning into the camera.

"Where was that taken?"

"Rav's wedding," said Kate.

"Oh."

There was another silence. Kate had the impression that Chloe was bracing herself to say something. "What?" she asked.

"Oh, nothing."

"No, come on. Spit it out."

Chloe looked at her. Then she put down her mug.

"It's nothing – it's none of my business anyway but – I was just wondering how things were going with Tin."

"With Tin?" Kate asked blankly.

Chloe looked uncomfortable. "It's just, I know you're going out to see him soon..."

With a jolt, Kate realised that her flight was fast approaching. She hadn't even started packing or getting currency or anything, really.

"Yes, that's right."

"Right. It's just – he wants you to move out there, right?"

"Yes." Kate was wondering where Chloe was going with this.

Chloe looked even more uncomfortable. "Are you – are you engaged to him?"

Kate was startled. "No."

"He hasn't asked you?"

"No," said Kate. She was aware of some sort of un-comfortable emotion beginning to unfold, tightening the pit of her stomach.

Chloe looked down at her hands. "Look, this really is none of my business," she said, almost in a mumble. "But – well, you're my friend, and I'd feel bad if I didn't say this. You can tell me to sod off, if you like. It's just – well—"

"Spit it out," Kate said again.

Chloe looked up. "I think if you go out there, *move* out there, and you're not married or even engaged, or have any sort of recognition from Tin about the sacrifice that you're making for him, I think you're in a very vulnerable position." She was silent for a moment and then added "That's all."

Kate blinked, trying to get a hold of her feelings. "That's *all*?"

Chloe dropped her gaze to her hands again. "That's just my opinion." She went quiet again and then burst out "Look, if you move out there, you're giving up your job, your house, your friends, your family, God knows what else, and for what? For a man who won't even make any kind of commitment to you? Christ, Kate, can't you see that?"

In the silence that followed, Merlin leapt up onto Kate's lap and curled himself into a comma shape, his black tail flicking.

"You're right," Kate said, after a long, uncomfortable silence.

"What?" said Chloe. Hope peeped into her expression.

"It's none of your business."

Chloe's face fell. "Well, yes, I know that—"

Kate struggled for a moment not to say something she'd regret. She found her hand stroking Merlin's silky black back compulsively, over and over again. It cost her something to say what she said. "I appreciate you giving me your thoughts."

Chloe managed a wry smile "But just sod off, eh?"

Kate breathed out, momentarily closing her eyes. "Look, I don't want to argue with you—"

"Well, me either—"

"Look, it's late. Let's—" She stopped herself from saying 'let's talk about it tomorrow'. She didn't want to talk about it to Chloe again, *ever*. "Let's leave it for now."

"Okay," Chloe said miserably. "Look, I'm sorry—"

Kate got up, dislodging Merlin. "Let's just – let's just forget it. Okay?"

"Okay."

They exchanged wan and awkward smiles. Then Chloe said, more formally, "Thanks for a nice evening."

"You're welcome."

"See you tomorrow, then."

Kate saw Chloe to the door and watched from the porch to see her get safely into her car. Chloe waved as she drove away, but her smile was still strained. Kate waved back and then closed and locked the front door. Then she stood in the darkened hallway, head bowed and breathing deeply, fighting the impulse to head-butt the door.

Chapter Ten

KATE WAS SOMEWHAT RELIEVED ON entering the office the next morning to see that Chloe wasn't at her desk. Briefly wondering where she was, Kate said good morning to Rav and Theo, waved at Olbeck, encased behind his glass office wall, and picked up the plastic folder of the print outs that Josh had given her yesterday. She'd made some progress the day before, but there was still more to do. She took herself off to an empty office, needing some peace and solitude to concentrate on the task.

After lunch, she headed for Olbeck's room and knocked at his door.

"Got a minute?"

"For you, Kate, anytime."

Kate grinned and sat down on the opposite side of his desk. She realised suddenly that last night had been the first time Olbeck and Jeff had managed to attend an adoption information evening together. She hastened to ask him how it had gone.

"Oh, fine, fine. I think so, anyway. There's still a

hell of a way to go, though." Olbeck rubbed a hand over his jaw. "I'm starting to get a bit nervous, actually." He caught Kate's eye and grinned sheepishly. "All right, a bit *more* nervous."

"You'll be fine," said z but they do still talk to one another through the website as well."

"Right."

"I think mermaid sixty-eight is a woman. No, I'm sure of it. She's obviously married, with several older children, because she mentions them briefly, now and again, in her messages."

Olbeck shuffled through the printouts, trying to read for himself. "Well, hopefully Josh or whoever will have found out who she is by now. Don't you need a credit card for signing up to this site? She should be easy to trace."

"Yes, I know. I'm heading down there now to see what's what."

"Great. Get me a name and we'll head straight out for an interview, if we can get hold of her."

Kate nodded and stood up, gathering together her papers. "There's just one thing..."

Olbeck looked up sharply. "What?"

"Well—" Kate hesitated. "It's just – if this mermaid sixty-eight is our killer, why wait six months to do it? They've been meeting in secret for that long. And why kill him? What's the motive?"

"Come on, Kate, we can't possible speculate about that until we actually see the woman."

"I know. It's just – that last message between the two of them. He's obviously going to get trussed up in all that stuff before she even arrives. So it's not as if he's afraid of her or anything." A thought suddenly struck Kate. "Hang on, can you even handcuff yourself without help? Remember that spy case in London, the one where that poor guy was found zipped into a bag?"

Olbeck made a puzzled face. "Eh?" Then his face cleared. "Oh yes, that one. Well that was dodgy as hell, wasn't it? Big cover-up by MI5, if you ask me. Anyway, given our case here, I doubt Simon Farraday could have snapped *both* those cuffs on by himself. Maybe he was just going to get as – well, immobilised as he could before she arrived?"

Kate made an impatient noise. "Well, anyway. That bit's probably not important. But Simon Farraday died because someone struck him on the head in a frenzy. As if they'd gone mad with rage. If that was this mermaid person, what on Earth did Simon Farraday say to her to make her react like that? Because if – *if* she'd targeted him for some reason of her own, and she was always planning to kill him – why *then*? Why like that?"

The two of them stared across the desk at one another for a long moment. Then Olbeck sagged back into his chair. "This case," he mumbled. "I tell you, I could do without it, right now."

"Tell me about it." Kate hugged the plastic folder to her. "And I'm off to New York at the end of the week."

Olbeck groaned aloud. "Oh, God, I'd forgotten. *Great*. Is anyone covering for you?"

"I thought Anderton was going to try and get someone on secondment while I'm away. It's only for five days."

"Five days!" Olbeck churned his hair with his hands in a manner reminiscent of Anderton. "Oh well, I'm sure we'll manage. I know you've had it booked for a long while. And you must be looking forward to seeing Tin."

"Oh yes," Kate said automatically, but after she said goodbye and went back to her desk, she wondered whether that was really the case. Of course I want to see him, she told herself, stealing a look at Chloe's empty desk. Curse her friend. She'd put all sorts of bad ideas into Kate's head. Then her innate sense of fairness made her reconsider. Was part of the reason she'd been so angry with Chloe because she knew, deep down, that Chloe was speaking sense?

With an irritated sigh, Kate flung the plastic folder onto the seat of her chair and made for the doorway, hoping that Josh had at least managed to find a name for their prime suspect.

As it happened, Josh was away from his computer. Sighing even more heavily, Kate left a Post-it note on his computer, had a quick look for Sam, who was also nowhere to be seen, and, shaking her head, climbed back up the stairs again to the office.

*

Chloe was back at her desk by that point, and she and Kate exchanged slightly embarrassed smiles as Kate sat back down again. There was a moment's awkward silence before Chloe cleared her throat. "Morning, bird."

"Morning. Bird," said Kate, unable to help a grin. "What's new?"

Theo looked up from his own desk. "I've been going back through all the CCTV footage. The whole of the past fortnight." He rubbed his eyes as if for emphasis. "Feel like I'm going blind."

"That won't be the CCTV footage," said Kate, getting up and giving him a wink. Theo laughed. Kate walked over to join him. "So, any more on our mysterious woman?"

"Nope. Nothing untoward at all. A couple of women go into the house the day before the murder but they're obviously the cleaners."

"Why 'obviously'?"

Theo gave her a look. "Because they're carrying mops and buckets and a vacuum cleaner? Anyway, they come out again after a couple of hours, and they're not seen again. There's no one, apart from Mia Farraday, on the morning of the day the crime was discovered, that even enters the house. Apart from the woman the night before."

Kate pulled up a chair and sat down next to Theo. "Let's see."

She waited as Theo tracked down the correct file and watched again as the grainy footage unfolded.

The two of them watched the blurry outline of the woman push open the front door of the townhouse and disappear from view.

"You've double checked the other camera, the one in the lane behind the house?" checked Kate.

Theo sighed. "Yes."

"Where did she go?" Kate asked, softly, almost to herself. Then she sat up a bit. "What about Simon Farraday?"

Theo looked at her in consternation. "What about him?"

Kate rolled her eyes. "Well, when did he get there, that night?"

Theo's expression gradually developed into that of a man who'd just realised he'd made a major *faux pas*. "Ah..." he began, uncertainly.

"Oh come *on*," said Kate. "Tell me you checked for him, too."

"Look, I've just about gone snow blind looking for this bloody bird. I haven't had a chance to check for matey yet—"

Kate looked at him. "Come on, Theo. Anderton's going to want to know, even if we don't. And we do."

"All right." She could tell by Theo's muttered tone that he was annoyed – probably more at himself than anyone else. Kindly, she refrained from uttering any more criticism and merely patted him on the shoulder as she got up.

As she walked back to her desk, her phone started

ringing. Chloe looked across to see if Kate was going to answer it, and seeing her colleague hurrying back to pick up the receiver, nodded to herself.

"Hello?" said Kate.

"Oh, hiya, it's Josh. I've got a name for you. Mermaid sixty-eight, you know."

"Yes, I know." Kate fought the urge to roll her eyes. "What is it, then?"

She wrote down the details Josh gave her, although he would put it all on an email as well. Kate didn't want to wait for that. She dashed back over to Olbeck's office, waving her bit of paper. He looked up so quickly that Kate realised he must have been subconsciously looking out for her all morning.

"You got it?" was all he said. Kate nodded, smiling. "Excellent. Come in here, then, and we'll see if we can get hold of her."

Chapter Eleven

"MELANIE HOUGHTON," SAID KATE, READING from a print out of the email that Josh had sent her an hour ago. She looked down at her lap as Olbeck drove them out of central Abbeyford and towards the suburb of Charlock, and the combination of reading and the car's motion was making her feel a little sick. She looked up and out of the window, winding it down a few inches to get some fresh air.

"You okay?"

"I'll be fine. I just can't read in cars."

"Well, you won't have to navigate." Olbeck looked at the changing image on the sat nav. "We'll be there in fifteen minutes."

Kate lay her head back against the headrest, breathing deeply and beginning to feel a bit better. "This is so *odd*, this case. I mean, it really is. If – if this Melanie is our killer, and she tracked Simon Farraday down for whatever reason of her own, why—" Kate broke off abruptly. "No, even that doesn't work. Simon

Farraday contacted *her*. Not the other way round." She rubbed her forehead in frustration.

"Look, stop flailing around for motives," Olbeck said in exasperation. "Motives are the least of our worries. We haven't even interviewed her yet."

"How did she sound on the phone?"

"Worried."

"Hmm."

"She also mentioned that her husband would be out. That might be of some importance."

"I'll say." Kate's phone chimed with an incoming text message. She read it, holding it up to the windscreen so she wouldn't have to look down. "That was from Chloe – forensic reports are in, apparently. She and Rav are going to make a start on them."

"Good," Olbeck said absently, occupied with following the sat nav's instructions. The suburb of Charlock was affluent and desirable, but the streets were lined on either side with cars, reducing the road to a single lane. Meeting a car coming the other way meant a game of 'who'll let who through first'. Olbeck cursed as the car facing them decided not to bother waiting and barged on through. "God, I *hate* it when people don't thank you for letting them go first."

"Go and arrest him," said Kate, grinning. "Give him a fright."

"I would, if I had the time," Olbeck said with emphasis. "Okay, here's number twenty-seven. I'll have to park further up."

*

AFTER INCHING THEIR WAY INTO a parking spot precisely three inches longer than Olbeck's car at either end, Kate and her colleague got out and prepared themselves for the knock at the door. It was always a moment of uncertainty. Were they coming face to face with a murderer? Or would they have to put an understandably terrified and embarrassed woman at her ease?

"Ready?" Olbeck straightened the cuffs of his suit. For a moment, Kate was swept with a pang of nostalgia for the time when he'd worn scruffy jeans and a fleece hoody, back when she'd first met him. "What's up?"

"Nothing. It just made me realise how smart you've got lately."

Olbeck grinned. "Well, I've got to look respectable now, haven't I?"

"Come on, Beau Brummel." Kate propelled him discreetly towards the black-painted door of twenty-seven Marlborough Avenue. Her flippant comment disguised a gradually growing sense of tension at the interview coming up.

The house was a terrace but one a long way removed from the terrace where Kate had grown up. This one was Edwardian, with a large bay window on the ground floor, potted bay trees to either side of the front door, a front garden modelled on a formal rose garden in miniature. Kate sized up the outside of the property. Terrace or no terrace, these babies were probably going for not much less than half a million pounds. What did Melanie Houghton do? If she was at home during the day, did that mean she didn't work outside of the home?

The front door was answered promptly, so quickly after Olbeck's knock of the shiny brass doorknocker, in fact, that Kate wondered whether Melanie Houghton had been waiting in the hallway, hovering, ready to pounce. She opened the door and immediately gave an embarrassed laugh.

"Oh! I thought you'd be in uniform, for some reason."

She was a woman who was probably in her late forties but could have passed for someone several years younger. Her hair was dark red and plentiful, arranged around her face in a flattering and expensively cut style. She wore discreet diamond studs in her ears and was dressed in well-cut black trousers and a grey cashmere top, cashmere so finely woven that Kate could only guess at what it had cost.

"Please, do come in." Melanie Houghton ushered them nervously through to a large, nicely furnished sitting room at the front of the house. She twitched the curtains so they were slightly more closed before seating herself on the edge of the grey velvet sofa. "Could I get you some tea? Coffee?"

Both Kate and Olbeck declined. "We're here because we're investigating the death of Simon

Farraday, Mrs Houghton. I explained that on the phone?"

Melanie Houghton smiled nervously but blankly. "Yes?"

"I understand he was a friend of yours?"

Melanie's eyelids, discreetly made up in shades of oyster and soot, blinked rapidly. "A friend? Of mine? No, no. No, I'm sorry, you're mistaken about that."

If they had been sitting opposite the woman in an interview room, Kate would have pressed her foot against Olbeck's in response to this remark. In full view of their suspect, she could do no such thing here but she could almost telepathically sense his thoughts. *So you say...*

"But you know who we're referring to?" Olbeck pressed on.

Melanie Houghton smiled again, rather dismissively. "Oh yes. Well, it's been in all the papers, hasn't it? Horrible thing. But I'm sorry, I don't see what it's got to do with me."

Olbeck cleared his throat. "You weren't friends with Mr Farraday? Or should I say, you weren't his lover?"

Melanie Houghton reared her head back as if Olbeck had spat in her face. "Me? Are you joking? You must be mad—"

Kate sighed and interrupted her. She could tell already that Melanie Houghton was a man's woman, which meant that Kate would take on the less sympathetic role, leaving Olbeck to be the good cop.

"Your credit card has been linked to a profile on an adult dating site, Mrs Houghton. The email address used in that profile corresponds to the internet server that powers the web access of this house." Melanie Houghton mouthed like a fish, and Kate felt a stab of pity for her, pity that was quickly dispersed by the woman's next remark.

"That must be a mistake," Melanie said in a hostile voice. "Someone must have hacked into my email address and...and set up that profile. It wasn't me."

Kate sighed audibly. This wasn't going to go well. Melanie Houghton obviously belonged to that large group of people who genuinely believed the police were stupid. It was almost insulting. "So no doubt somebody stole your credit card as well, Mrs Houghton?"

"That's right," Melanie said stubbornly. Her gaze dropped to her lap, where her well-manicured hands were shaking.

Kate looked across at Olbeck. He dropped her the ghost of a wink and turned back to the other woman. "Well, here's the thing, Mrs Houghton. We can either ask you some questions here, in the privacy of your own home, or we can arrest you and you'll have to accompany us down to the police station, where we can interview there. What's it to be?"

Melanie Houghton almost gagged. White-faced, she gasped "You – you can't – you can't do that—"

"I'm afraid we can, Mrs Houghton." Olbeck's tone grew steely. "This is a murder enquiry."

"Oh god. Oh my god." Melanie Houghton's composure had utterly vanished. She dropped her head into her hands and burst into tears. "Please – please don't—"

"Will you talk to us here?"

"Yes – yes, my god—" She appeared to make a mammoth effort to control herself. "I'm sorry if I – I didn't mean—"

Kate couldn't bear any more. "Let's get on with it, Mrs Houghton, shall we?" She glanced across at Olbeck, for his permission to continue, and then leant forward a little, beginning her questions.

*

MELANIE HOUGHTON HAD ONE OF those complexions which crying really didn't suit. After twenty minutes of halting confession, embarrassed recollection and hesitation, Mrs Houghton's eyelids matched the red of her hair and her nose was running so much that she held a tissue under it almost permanently.

"I'm not expecting you to understand," she said eventually, her voice thick with tears. "I'm not trying to excuse myself. Well, perhaps I am." She raised her head for a moment and fixed them both with a glare. "We've been married for over twenty-five years. Do you know what that's like? The tedium, the *boredom*. Constantly knowing what the other's going to say? Sitting across from one another in restaurants, listening to one another *chew*. And as for sex—" She broke off, crumpling the sodden tissue in one hand. "Well, suffice to say that *that* falls by the wayside, a lot sooner than you might think."

From her earlier reticence, Melanie Houghton was a changed woman. Kate had seen this happen before in interviews – the mood changed to something almost approaching a therapy session, at least on behalf of the suspect. Looking at Melanie, she could imagine the woman had had her fair share of psychoanalysis. There was something tightly wound about her, something that the expensive clothing, the diamond earrings, the musky perfume couldn't quite hide. Kate continued to listen to her talk, blurt, even, with a twinge of unease.

Eventually Melanie fell silent, her chest rising in an occasional hitching breath as she recovered herself from her crying fit. Olbeck cleared his throat. "Mrs Houghton, you say that you've been meeting Simon Farraday for some months, since November last year, both here at your house and at Mr Farraday's townhouse. Is that correct?" Melanie nodded, her eyes downcast. "So can you confirm the last time you saw Mr Farraday?"

Melanie kept her eyes down low. "I don't remember exactly. It was about two weeks ago."

Kate stiffened. She heard Olbeck ask in a steady

tone "About two weeks ago? You didn't meet up with him on the night of the ninth of April?"

Olbeck's tone was entirely neutral – he was too experienced an interviewer to betray any emotion at a startling piece of news – but something intangible must have alerted Melanie Houghton who sat up, compulsively crushing the tissue in her hand. "What do you mean? The night of the ninth of April?"

"Yes. Didn't you meet him at the Farradays' townhouse that night?"

Melanie was staring. "No. No, I didn't." The date that Olbeck had mentioned must have struck a chord because she blanched and said "Wasn't that – was that the night—"

"He was killed? Yes," Olbeck said, looking at her steadily.

"He – that – no, no, I didn't, I didn't." Kate held herself more tensely. Melanie Houghton's tone held a note of increasing hysteria. "I didn't!"

"Okay, okay, it's all right, Mrs Houghton." Olbeck broke eye contact and looked down. The tension in the room lessened very slightly. "Where were you on the night of the ninth of April, between the hours of ten pm and midnight?"

"I – I—" Melanie Houghton must have realised by that point that she was a suspect. Her tone began to climb ever higher. "I – I don't – I don't—"

Kate was on the edge of her seat now. She'd seen that stance before, the coiled spring intensity of a person close to the edge. She could feel Olbeck tense beside her.

As if a balloon had suddenly popped inside her, Melanie Houghton sagged back against the back of the velvet sofa. A look of intense relief came into her face. "I was here," she murmured. "I was here with my husband. We were watching television – it was the last episode of *The Mother Trap* – I remember now. We were here, I was here. Oh—" She covered her face with her hands, crying again.

Kate and Olbeck exchanged a glance. Olbeck cleared his throat. "We will have to interview your husband, Mrs Houghton. He will have to confirm what you've just told us."

Melanie's hands dropped away from her face. The look of relief was gone and the whiteness of her skin shone out in pallid contrast to her glorious hair. "Oh," was all she said, feebly.

"We'll call back this evening, Mrs Houghton." Olbeck shifted himself forward on the sofa, preparatory to getting up. "I presume your husband will be home later?" Melanie nodded, as if all the strength had gone out of her muscles. "Well, that should give you a chance to talk to him before we get here. Shall we say about seven o'clock?" Another feeble nod from the mistress of the house. "Very well. We'll talk again then. We'll see ourselves out."

*

THEY WERE IN THE CAR before either Kate or Olbeck

said anything. Then Kate blew out her cheeks and rolled her eyes.

"I know," said Olbeck. He frowned for a moment and then reached for his phone. Kate heard him dialling and then speaking to someone who sounded like Rav.

"Going to put a watch on her?" Kate asked, having listened to Olbeck's half of the conversation.

"Yes. I don't know, it might be a bit over cautious but..." He didn't elaborate but his words fell away in a sigh. "Well, I don't know about you, but there's something about that woman that makes me uneasy."

"I know what you mean," Kate said with feeling. "You don't think she's going to cut and run, do you?"

Olbeck shrugged. "No. No, it's not that. It's just *something* – did she strike you as – not quite right?" He turned on the ignition and began the slow, painful process of edging out of the parking space. "Without exactly being able to say what was wrong with her?"

Kate rubbed her chin. "You know who she reminded me of?"

"Who?"

"Elodie Duncan's mother. What was her name? Genevieve Duncan."

"Mm. Maybe you're right. So do you think she was lying about meeting him on the night of the murder?"

It was Kate's turn to shrug. "Not sure. That's something we'll have to look into. Let's see what the husband says later."

"Right." Olbeck had manoeuvred out onto the road by this point. "Lord, I don't envy her *that* conversation later."

Kate said nothing but made a heartfelt noise in agreement.

Chapter Twelve

"So," Anderton said the next morning, pacing backward and forwards across the office floor. "Where are we so far?"

Kate leant back and swung her legs, wondering whether she was going to be the first person to speak. As it was, Theo beat her to it.

"I've been looking at the CCTV footage from the scene, both of the front door of the townhouse and the back lane that runs behind it." Anderton nodded encouragingly. "Well, we've ascertained that Simon Farraday was the first person to enter the house, on the night of the ninth of April, at about seven thirty. Then there's absolutely nothing until the woman, who we haven't been able to identify, enters the front door at nine fifty-three pm."

Theo paused. Anderton raised his eyebrows expectantly. "And?"

Theo looked a little awkward. "Well, the problem is that she doesn't come out."

"Come again?" Anderton said, pausing in his journey back and forth across the carpet.

"She doesn't come out. Either through the back door or through the front door."

Anderton gave Theo an expressive look. "What? So where does she go?"

Theo looked even more awkward. "Well, that's just it. There's no footage of her leaving, not that night or the next morning."

Kate cleared her throat. "Theo, the blank spot – remember?"

"I was just about to get to that." Theo gave her an annoyed look. "There's an interval of about fifteen minutes at about two am in the morning when the tape goes on the fritz. It's possible that she may have left then."

Anderton threw his hands in the air. "Possible? Of course it's bloody possible! What's the alternative? That she teleported out of there? Walked through a bloody wall?" Kate suppressed a giggle just as Anderton came to a sudden halt, staring ahead of him.

There was a tense silence while the team waited for him to speak again. Then he came back to life and pointed at Theo. "Get onto the Land Registry. You need to get hold of the floor plan for the Farradays' townhouse."

"What—" Theo began but Kate had already grasped the implications.

"He's saying – sorry, sir, *you're* saying – that there

might be another way out of the house? Something we aren't yet aware of?"

"A secret tunnel?" Chloe asked in a cynical voice.

Anderton smiled, unoffended. "Something like that. That house is *old*. I'm thinking priest hole, walled up cellar, something like that. Someone will need to go and interview Mia Farraday again, see if she can shed any light on the matter."

"I'll do the Land Registry," said Theo.

"I'm happy to talk to Mia Farraday," said Kate.

"Good." Anderton clapped his hands together in satisfaction. "Disappearing women, I don't know. You lot are supposed to be professionals." The team exchanged guilty smiles. "Now, what else? Chloe, Rav, anything from forensics?"

Chloe grabbed for a pile of cardboard folders. "Yes, we started going through them yesterday. As luck would have it, the townhouse was cleaned just before the day of the murder so there were only a few fingerprints found. Prints from Mia and Simon Farraday, as you'd expect, the cleaning ladies and—" She paused for dramatic effect. "The fingerprints of an unknown woman were found in the bedroom of the house."

By now Olbeck had joined the conference. "We've asked Melanie Houghton, Simon Farraday's lover, to come to the station today to be fingerprinted. It wouldn't surprise me to find that she's the unknown woman."

"Good," said Anderton.

"Actually, I wouldn't mind five minutes after this for a quick chat," said Olbeck. He looked across at Kate and mouthed 'you too'. She raised her eyebrows but nodded.

"Sure, sure." Anderton rubbed his jaw, staring at the whiteboards on the far wall, which were covered in black marker scribbles, arrows, photographs and notes. "I've got half an hour before I have to nip out to a meeting, so come down to my office." He swept the room with his gaze. "Anybody else have anything?"

"I'm going to check with IT whether they've managed to track down all the other online contacts Simon Farraday was in correspondence with," said Kate. "They'll all need to be interviewed as well."

"Good. Keep me posted. Anyone else?" There was a short silence and a general shaking of heads and muttering of 'no, nothing'. "Good. Keep up the good work and we'll reconvene later."

The team dispersed, and Olbeck walked over to where Kate was sitting.

"What's all this about?" Kate asked, but she had a pretty good idea.

"I want to talk to Anderton about our interview with the Houghtons last night."

Kate nodded. She'd been right in her supposition. "Thought so. Come on, then."

*

ANDERTON'S OFFICE FELT SMALLER THAN usual,

due to the exercise bike that had taken up station over by the window. This was a new fad of Anderton's, although no one had actually ever seen him use it. According to office gossip, he arrived before anyone else in the morning in order to take his half hour of exercise then.

Kate found her gaze moving from the bike to Anderton's undeniably trimmer figure. Feeling suddenly hot, she switched her gaze and tried to focus on what Olbeck was saying.

"There's something really odd about that couple," he told Anderton. "They look perfectly normal but there's – I don't know – an undercurrent of something weird in their relationship. I can't put my finger on what, though."

Anderton snorted. "The fact that the man's coming to terms with his missus having been banging some other bloke trussed up in black leather?"

Olbeck grinned sheepishly. "Well, I suppose there's that."

"Presumably we're finger printing them both, of course?"

"Of course. They're both suspects. He has even more of a motive than she does."

Kate repressed the impulse to say 'motives are the least of our worries'. Instead she leant forward a little and said "Neither of the Houghtons has an alibi, except for the one they're giving each other."

"Which means they're pretty much worthless."

Anderton leant back in his chair and laced his fingers behind his head. Kate averted her eyes from the swell of muscle pushing against the white cotton of his shirt. What was the matter with her? Keep your mind on the job, she told herself sternly. You're going to see your *boyfriend* in a couple of days. Anderton was still speaking. "That missing fifteen minutes on the CCTV—"

"Yes?" asked Olbeck.

"Well, isn't it entirely possible that the murderer entered the house, killed Farraday and left again in that short space of time?"

There was a moment when they all considered this, and then Olbeck shook his head. "The timing doesn't work. Medical evidence says Farraday was dead before midnight."

"Damn it." Anderton took his hands down again and sat forward. "We're not getting anywhere with this. It could be that the woman we see on the tape is the murderer but she also had an accomplice and that both of them leave the house in that missing fifteen minutes."

Kate stared at him. "Should we bring the Houghtons in for questioning?"

"Well, they're coming in already, aren't they?" Anderton rubbed his jaw in thought for a moment. "Yes. Bring them in. They're not under arrest – yet – but I want to speak to them. I'll do the interview, so just make sure you let me know when they're ready for me."

Kate opened her mouth to ask if she could sit in on that when she realised she was due to question Mia Farraday that morning. She repressed a sharp jab of disappointment.

"I'll do that," said Olbeck.

"Good. Right, I've got to go. I'll see you two later."

Olbeck and Kate got up to leave when something else occurred to Kate. "I've just thought of something."

"Yes?" Both men looked at her enquiringly.

"The – the bondage gear. If the murderer was wearing it as well, I mean. Wouldn't that be a good way of covering up – I mean, making sure you minimised the chances of dropping hair and skin. Keeping it clean for the forensics, I mean."

There was a short silence. "Well, it's an idea," Anderton said, doubt edging his voice. "It's an idea..."

"Oh, forget it," said Kate. "I was just thinking aloud, that's all."

*

BACK IN THE CORRIDOR AND walking back to the office, Kate stopped and put a hand on Olbeck's sleeve.

"What is it?"

Kate paused, chewing her lip. "This case – do you get the impression... " She stopped, unsure of exactly what she wanted to say.

"What is it?" asked Olbeck again.

Kate sighed. "You know at first we thought it might be really simple, and then we realised it really wasn't?"

"Yes?"

"Well—" She stopped again, frustrated by her inability to articulate what she was feeling. "I think – it has the feel of something that *seems* one way but is actually the other."

"Sorry," said Olbeck, looking mystified. "You've lost me."

Kate exhaled. "Oh, it's nothing. I don't even know what I'm trying to say."

"Never mind," said Olbeck, kind as always. "I'm sure everything will seem a lot clearer soon."

"I hope you're right."

They started walking again. "You're off to New York on Friday, aren't you?" Olbeck asked.

"Yes, that's right." Kate wondered why she didn't feel as excited as she thought she should be. "I can't wait," she added, wondering who she was convincing.

"You'll love it. It's a great city." They'd reached the office door by now, and Olbeck courteously stood back to let Kate go through first. "Bet you can't wait to see Tin again."

"That's right," Kate said, and this time she was relieved to find that she sounded like she actually meant it.

Chapter Thirteen

As it happened, Kate wasn't able to pin down a meeting with Mia Farraday until that evening. She made the appointment and noted it down, beginning to feel the first stirrings of panic that her overseas trip began in less than two days and she hadn't packed, sorted out her house, ordered some dollars or, in fact, done anything to prepare. Oh, one thing was done – Merlin was taken care of. Both Olbeck and Chloe had offered to feed and water him over the time Kate was away. Quickly, Kate scribbled a list of things to be done and crossed out 'Merlin' with a flourish of satisfaction.

It had been a day of grey skies and rain but the temperature was surprisingly high. Very muggy, thought Kate, winding down her car window as she drove away from the station. The sort of weather that preceded a thunderstorm. She made a mental note to check what the weather in New York was going to be like over the weekend. She didn't want to be packing sun dresses and flip-flops if it was going to be in minus temperatures.

The countryside was even more lushly green than it had been when Kate and Olbeck had first driven to the Farraday residence. Days of mingled rain and sunshine had meant the hedges and trees and grasses were growing with verdant abandon. The air flowing through Kate's open window was heavy with the fresh smells of new growth and tree blossom. Now that the clocks had gone forward, it was still light at almost eight o'clock in the evening.

All of it put her in a cheerful mood. She parked the car outside the Farradays' house, noting that there were no cars in sight at all today. Mandy, the WPC liaison officer, must have been moved on.

Sarah Collins opened the door to Kate. Quickly observant, Kate noted the flash of unease that briefly crossed the girl's features at the sight of her.

"Good evening," she said, brightly. "I have an appointment to see Mrs Farraday."

"I—" Sarah began, but there was movement behind her and Mia Farraday came into view, toddler Tilly settled on her hip.

"That's fine, Sarah, let DS Redman in." Mia sounded less cross than resigned. "Can you go and take over upstairs?" She handed Tilly over to Sarah, the little girl beginning to whine and hold out her chubby arms. "Oh, shush, Tilly, I won't be a moment." She beckoned Kate through to a room she hadn't been in before, a study cum office at the side of the house. "The boys are just finishing their bath," Mia explained, as Sarah disappeared from view, Tilly's complaints trailing behind her.

"I'm sorry to interrupt you all—" Kate began, but Mia waved a hand in dismissal.

"It's fine, it's fine, I understand." She shut the study door and seated herself opposite Kate, looking at her expectantly. "How can I help?"

Kate crossed her legs. "Mrs Farraday, can you tell me if there's an – an alternative exit to the two doors in the townhouse?"

Mia looked blank. "Sorry?"

Kate explained more fully, without mentioning the CCTV issue. Mia's face cleared. "Oh. I see. Well, I'm not sure. I don't remember anything like that."

"You don't remember seeing anything on the floor plans, or when you bought the house?" Mia shook her head slowly. "When did you buy the house, Mrs Farraday?"

"Oh, gosh. Years ago. Actually, Simon bought it before I married him. It was one of his first properties. I don't remember ever actually seeing a floor plan or anything like that."

"I understand. Would you know if your husband kept any papers relating to the purchase, or anything like that?" Kate knew that the Land Registry would have a copy of anything relevant, but it might save time if she could get hold of a floor plan now. It would also really annoy Theo, which meant, let's face it, an added bonus. Kate realised she was grinning at the thought and quickly adjusted her face.

"I'm not sure. I think anything like that would probably be in here. This is where we keep all the paperwork."

She was still using the present tense when referring to her husband, Kate noticed. Not that that was unusual. In fact, it was more suspicious when people quickly started using the past tense.

Kate knew that the house would have been searched already but she got up and went over to where Mia was standing by an open filing cabinet. "May I?" she asked, reaching out towards the files.

"Of course. Please, help yourself."

Kate quickly flicked through the files. It was mostly made up of indeterminably dull business papers, household accounts and utility bills. She couldn't find anything like a floor plan for the town house. Oh well, Theo would have to get the glory this time.

"Thank you," she said, trying not to let the disappointment show in her tone.

Mia nodded but said nothing. She was shifting a little from foot to foot. "Will that be all, Detective Sergeant? Because I really should be putting the kids to bed..."

"Yes. Yes, sorry." Kate straightened up and smiled. "Don't let me keep you. I know you've got your hands full."

"Haven't I just? But I love it. I love being a mum." Mia's slender face softened. "I would have liked more, you know."

"Really?" said Kate, to be polite and also because she was interested. She didn't really know of anyone who had more than three children. Apart from her own mother, of course. "I'm one of six myself."

"Six? How lovely." Kate smiled non-committally. Mia went on. "Yes, I would have loved a really big family."

She stopped talking abruptly. After a moment, Kate said, prompting, "Yes?"

Mia sighed. "Yes. But Simon didn't want any more. I had to fight him to have Tilly, to be honest. And then after she was born, he came home one day and said 'I'm having a vasectomy next week,' and that was that."

"Just like that?" Kate asked, shocked.

Mia smiled sadly. "Just like that."

"He didn't – you didn't discuss it, or anything like that?"

Mia half laughed. "No, we didn't. Simon wasn't like that. He just decided and went out and had it done. No matter what I thought or wanted."

Kate struggled to find the appropriate words for a moment. "Well, I'm sorry to hear that," was what she managed to come up with, eventually.

Mia shrugged. "Thank you. It's fine, though. I've got my three." There were faint yells from upstairs and she began to walk towards the door. "Oh, heavens, I'd better go. Sorry—"

"I'll see myself out," said Kate. "Thank you, Mrs Farraday."

Mia gave her a harassed smile as she headed off towards the stairs. Kate raised a hand in farewell and headed towards the front door.

A shout from Mia made her pause and turn back. "Yes?"

Mia was hanging over the banisters of the stairs. "I've just had a thought. If you want to know about the townhouse, you'd do worse than talk to Ewan Askell. He's really hot on local history and architecture."

"Ewan Askell?" Kate recalled Simon Farraday's deputy. "Is he?"

"Yes, he's chairman of some sort of local history club, but I remember him talking to Simon one day about the townhouse and its history. He might know about it if anyone would." The yells from upstairs increased and Mia rolled her eyes. "Sorry, I'm really going to have to go—"

"That's fine. Thank you." Kate watched her run up the stairs out of sight and then turned to let herself out of the front door.

*

The heavy door closed behind her, cutting off the noise and the tumult of the Farraday children's bedtime routine, Kate walked along the little bridge that led across the water feature. Waterlilies were beginning to open their creamy white flowers, each trembling petal reflected in the water below. Kate clicked the button on her key fob to open her car door and got in, thinking about what Mia had just said.

Now she remembered Olbeck telling her about Ewan Askell's alibi on the night of Simon Farraday's death. *He was at some local history society meeting that night and he gave one of his fellow historians a lift home and didn't get back to his own place until well after midnight. So, it's* unlikely *he was involved, but...*

Kate put the car into gear and drove off, frowning. It was beginning to rain again, and dusk was seeping into the evening air. So, Ewan Askell was a bit of a local history buff, was he? There was something there that chimed with something else that Kate had been told. What was it? Something to do with Mia Farraday. Oh, that was right – Mia had studied history at university. Was that significant? Or just a coincidence? Kate found herself wondering how well Mia and Ewan Askell knew each other. She hadn't got the impression from Mia that he was anything other than a colleague of her husband's, but there had been something in Ewan's voice when he'd mentioned Mia that now made Kate pause, thinking back. Had there? Or was she imagining things?

It was dark enough by now to need the car headlights on. Kate flipped the switch and pressed the accelerator, wanting now to get home and get on with things before it got too late. She pushed the thoughts of the case to the back of her mind, needing to concentrate on other, more domestic worries.

Chapter Fourteen

"WELL, THEN," OLBECK SAID FOR the third time in the past half hour. "Got everything? Tickets, money, passport?"

"Yes," said Kate. "As I've said before, several times."

"Sorry." Olbeck gave her a sheepish grin. "I think I'm more nervous than you."

"What have you got to be nervous about?"

Olbeck began to pull Kate's carry-on bag along the floor, heading for the Departures gate. "I hate flying."

"Do you?" Kate asked, surprised.

"Yes. Absolutely hate it. I got so wound up about it when Jeff and I went to South Africa that I had to get some sedatives from the doctor before we went."

"*Really*?"

"Yes. A couple of Valium, and a stiff gin and tonic, and I was out for the count for most of the flight."

"What fun for Jeff." Kate panted after her friend, his long legs outpacing hers. "Look, hold up a minute. It's another hour until I have to board."

"Okay. How about a coffee?"

"Excellent idea," Kate said, wheezing.

*

THEY MANOEUVRED THEIR WAY THROUGH the crowded café, steering Kate's case around other, bulkier suitcases, until they managed to commandeer a small table towards the back. Kate collapsed into her seat with a sigh. Despite her outwardly calm demeanour, she was actually starting to feel a little anxious. It was not so much the thought of the trans-Atlantic flight as it was at the thought of seeing Tin again after so long. Of course, they'd called and Skyped and texted, and had even written postcards, but still...

"Look, don't worry if it's a bit awkward at first," Olbeck said, clearly reading her mind. "It's been a while since you've been together, and you've got a whole new city to contend with."

"I know." Their coffees had arrived commendably promptly, and Kate took a grateful pull of hers. "I'm sure we'll be fine."

"God, from a totally selfish point of view, I really wish you weren't going. This case is going to be one of those that just drags on and on, I can just feel it."

"Yes, well, don't go solving it without me," Kate said with a smile. "Anyway, I'm going to be checking in every day to see what I'm missing."

"Oh, don't do that – you're on holiday. I was only joking."

"Me too," Kate said with an awkward laugh, because she actually hadn't been. "But I might call in now and again, just to see how things are going."

"Okay. That would be great."

"Do we have anything from the Land Registry yet?" Kate hadn't been in the office for a day, occupied as she had been with trying to sort out everything at home.

Olbeck raised a finger. "Aha! Wait just one minute." He reached for the briefcase he'd carried with him since he'd picked Kate up that morning. "Now, I have it right here. Where is it?" He poked about in the papers within the case and extracted one. "Right, here we go. Take a look at this."

Kate followed the line of his pointing finger. "Wow. Anderton was right."

Olbeck nodded. "There's a passageway that runs from the cellar out to a sort of shed just around the corner. Coincidentally – or not – just out of reach of the CCTV camera that covers the back lane."

Kate pursed up her lips in a silent whistle. "So anyone who knew about it could just slip down to the cellar and leave the house that way?"

"Looks like it."

Kate sat back and looked at Olbeck. "So presumably that's how our mystery woman left the building? So she had to know about it?"

Olbeck lifted one shoulder. "Most probably, but the big problem we've got is that fifteen minutes when the CCTV tape went on the fritz. The murderer could have exited via this passageway or they could have left by the front door in the window of time where there was no footage."

Kate shook her head in frustration. "Is there a possibility that someone could have tampered with the CCTV? Is that why it went wrong?"

"No. Not unless they also had access to the council offices and the highly secure space where the CCTV is monitored. It's just too unlikely *and* the council have confirmed that it was an electrical fault that wiped off that fifteen minutes."

"Hmm." Kate bent over the floor plan again, tracing the outline of the passageway with her finger. "I'll tell you what else is a problem."

"What?"

Kate tapped the paper. "Why, *if* our murderer is this woman, and *if* she left the building by the passageway, why on Earth didn't she come *in* that way and stay off the CCTV completely?"

Olbeck's jaw dropped momentarily. "Bloody hell. That's a very good point." Kate sat back in satisfaction, just as the airport tannoy began to announce that her flight was boarding. "Oh, hell, you'd better go. You've still got to clear Security and everything, and you know how long *that* takes nowadays."

"Yes, I suppose so." Kate began to gather her belongings together with some regret. What she really wanted to do was keep talking the case over. *Come on, woman, try to feel a little excited...*

*

BY THIS TIME, IT WAS so late that there was no time other than to say a hurried goodbye at the departure gates and then deal with all the stress and fuss of Security, Passport Control and waiting to board the plane. It wasn't until Kate was sitting in her window seat, her handbag tucked neatly under the seat in front of her and a gin and tonic fizzing gently on the little table before her, that she finally felt able to relax. As the plane had taken off, she'd peered out, wondering with amusement whether one of the tiny coloured dots that were the cars on the motorway was Olbeck heading back to Abbeyford.

Kate sat back in her seat and took a sip of her drink. She was facing the prospect of a seven-hour flight and wondered what to do with herself. Before leaving, she'd loaded up her Kindle with several new books – should she read one of those? One was a new bestseller that Chloe had been raving about – perhaps she would start with that one. She leant forward for her handbag and then sat back again. On second thoughts, she didn't feel much like reading. She opened up the in-flight magazine and took a look at the films the airline was showing. Definitely a few there that she might watch. Kate slowly unwrapped the little plastic packet that contained her headphones. Then she closed up the packet again and put it back in the pocket on the back of the seat in front of her. She reached for her handbag, but instead of her Kindle, she took out a notebook and pen.

You're supposed to be on holiday, she told herself, but still she found herself beginning to scribble down some thoughts on the Farraday case. She wrote *CCTV issue – why did woman not use secret entrance to come into house as well as leave? Did she want to be seen on CCTV – why? WHO IS THIS WOMAN? NB. Check with Theo on fingerprints of other lovers.*

Kate paused for a moment, tapping her chin with her pen. Then she began to write again. *Who was Simon Farraday?*

She put her pen down and stared at what she'd written. What exactly did she mean by that? Kate frowned, thinking. There was that internal itch once more, the idea that the case was one thing while actually being another. Smoke and mirrors.

She began to write again, slowly, more of a jotting down of her stream of consciousness rather than an ordered series of notes. *If Melanie Houghton is woman on CCTV, she must know about secret exit or she happened to leave in 15 mins of tape on fritz. But could not have predicted that, surely? NB. Double check alibi.* Kate then remembered that Mr Houghton – what was his name? Jeremy Houghton – had alibied his wife. And she had done the same for him. Did that mean anything? Kate scribbled again. *Check J Houghton's fingerprints at townhouse – found?*

Kate stopped, catching her breath. Something else

had just occurred to her. Quickly, before she could forget it or get muddled, she wrote it down. *What if woman ISN'T murderer but OTHER killer entered and exited by secret tunnel so we don't see them at all?*

Kate clenched her hands with excitement. God, if only she weren't stuck on a plane... All she wanted to do was call Anderton and tell him her new theory, even if she hadn't had much time to reflect on it. If there had been another killer, who could it have been? Again, her thoughts went to the Houghtons and their mirror alibis. Was one of them shielding the other? But then, if Jeremy Houghton had killed Simon Farraday, where was the evidence and why would his wife, who had evidently been Simon's lover for months, let her husband get away with it?

Kate looked back over what she'd written, her eyes resting on a particular phase. *Who was Simon Farraday?*

Why did she feel that this was the key to the whole case? Was there something in Simon Farraday's past, an injury to someone, a misdemeanour, even a crime? Had the sins of the past finally caught up with him? But what, if anything, had he done? And why, if the murder was the result of a long-held hatred, had he been killed *now*?

Slowly Kate wrote a few more sentences. *Look into Farraday's past. Old friends?* She thought of those other women he'd been in contact with. Was one of them not who she seemed? Kate wrote a bullet-pointed list. *CCTV. Fingerprints. History. Houghtons' past and marriage.* She looked back at the word *History* and wrote *Ewan Askell* and added a question mark. Then she put down her pen.

Kate's head was beginning to hurt. She rubbed her temples, took a deep breath and closed her notebook, putting it back in her bag. Then she tipped the last flat, warm mouthful of her gin and tonic into her mouth and began to search for a film to watch, determined to try and leave the job behind, if only for a few days.

Chapter Fifteen

OLBECK WAS WALKING PAST ANDERTON'S office the next morning when he was startled, first by a shout, and secondly by his boss abruptly popping his head around the doorframe. "Mark! Got a minute?"

Obediently, Olbeck turned into Anderton's office and took a seat.

"Did Kate land okay?" was Anderton's first, rather anxious enquiry.

"Yes, she's fine, she sent me a text."

"Good." Anderton, who'd sat back down in his chair in the meantime, shuffled some papers on his desk.

"Was it anything urgent?" Olbeck enquired politely, after the seconds stretched out into silence.

"Oh, not really. Well, just wanted an update, if you've got one."

"On the Farraday case?"

"Yes," Anderton said impatiently. "I didn't mean the hunt for Lord bloody Lucan. What have we got so far?"

Repressing a smile, Olbeck sat forward a little.

"Right. Well. We've identified all six of the women contacted on the 4Adults website by Simon Farraday and interviewed them all. There's nothing to suggest that there was anything suspicious about any of them but naturally we've swabbed and fingerprinted them all, just for purposes of elimination."

Anderton nodded. "Good. Talking of fingerprints, have we got final confirmation on the ones found at the scene?"

"Yes. Off the top of my head, the only ones found were those of Mia and Simon Farraday, the two cleaning ladies and Melanie Houghton." Olbeck paused for effect. "And several from Ewan Askell."

Anderton stilled. "Ewan Askell being Simon Farraday's business partner?"

"His deputy."

"I see. What's his explanation for his prints being found there?"

"He seemed quite unruffled by it when we asked him. Said he'd dropped in with Simon on the way back from a meeting, so Simon could pick up some paperwork. They had a cup of coffee there, apparently, and Askell's prints were found in the kitchen, so I suppose it's plausible."

Anderton's eyes narrowed. "I thought the whole place had been cleaned the day before? When did Askell say he'd been there?"

"About a week before. I know, I know, why would his prints still be there, but I suppose it's possible that the cleaners missed that bit. Certainly, a defence lawyer could plausibly argue that his prints were there quite innocently."

"Hmm." Olbeck watched Anderton shuffle his paperwork again, obviously mindlessly as he thought of something else. "Have you asked him about this mysterious bloody tunnel yet?"

"Not yet. Rav is following that up today."

"Right." Anderton gave up on the paperwork and sat back in his chair. "So Melanie Houghton's prints were found on the scene, eh? In the bedroom, no doubt?"

Olbeck grinned. "That's right."

"Hmm. It's not looking too good for Mrs Houghton, is it? I've a good mind to pull her in again, under caution this time. There's DNA evidence linking her to the scene, she was emotionally and sexually involved with our murder victim, and her alibi's as weak as water." Something seemed to strike him. "No prints found from her old man, I suppose?"

"Jeremy Houghton? In the townhouse? No, nothing."

"Hmm." Anderton drummed his fingers on the desk. "I wonder. What did young Kate say about covering up to evade forensic detection?"

"Sorry?"

"Oh, I'm just thinking aloud. Kate mentioned something about the bondage gear being an effective way to make sure you didn't leave any DNA behind.

Something like that, anyway. I didn't think much of it at the time but..." He trailed off, rubbing his jaw. "Mark - do you get the impression that there's something behind this one, this case, that we're not quite seeing? That it's not quite what is seems?"

Olbeck stared at him. Then he said, doubtfully, "I suppose so. Nothing ever is just as it seems in a murder case, is it?"

Anderton sighed. "I know that. But—"

"It's funny you mentioning that, actually, because Kate said just the same thing."

"Did she now? She'll go far, that one." Anderton looked as if he were about to say more when the chime of an incoming email sounded on his computer and distracted him. "What's this? Christ, talk of the devil." He indicated his computer screen. "Young madam's just sent me an email."

"Kate?" Olbeck got up and walked around Anderton's desk to take a closer look. "She's emailing you now?" He did a quick mental calculation. "She must be mad. Isn't it about five thirty am over there at the moment?"

Anderton chuckled. "She's probably jetlagged. Besides, Americans start work ridiculously bloody early. She's picking up bad habits."

Both men read through the email in silence. After they'd finished, Anderton turned to Olbeck with his eyebrows raised. "Well. Do you think she has a point?"

"The fact that someone else could have entered

and exited the house without being seen at all? Yes, I suppose so." Olbeck was uneasily aware of the fact that he should have been able to pick that one up for himself. "But say she is right. How on Earth are we going to prove it?"

Anderton swung his chair round and grabbed a pen. He stabbed it at a piece of paper, marking out three bullet points. "Right, well, let's make a start. I want the Houghtons' house searched. Today. I'll organise the warrant. I want that CCTV footage sent off to a specialist to see if they can identify the woman on it. And I want Ewan Askell, Jeremy and Melanie Houghton in for further questioning. Got that?"

"Got it," Olbeck said, taking the note from his boss and trying not to droop at the thought of all the extra work ahead of him. Come back soon, Kate, he pleaded silently inside his head, wondering what his friend was up to over on the other side of the Atlantic. He hoped she was having fun, although seeing as she was up and sending work emails at the crack of dawn, that didn't bode particularly well.

Dismissing those thoughts, he took his leave of Anderton and made his way to the office, head filled with everything he had to set in motion today.

Chapter Sixteen

"What *are* you doing?"

Kate turned around from the glass-topped table that stood in one corner of Tin's living room. "Nothing much. Just catching up on emails. Did I wake you?"

"No, but – it's six o'clock in the morning, sweetheart. You shouldn't be working. Come back to bed."

Obediently, Kate got up. She'd sent the most important message already, the one to Anderton, and there was nothing to do now but wait until he replied. And, she reminded herself guiltily, I'm supposed to be here to spend time with Tin. Not to be preoccupied with work.

A couple of hours later, the two of them were showered and dressed and ready for breakfast. Tin had astonished Kate by claiming that he almost never ate in his apartment but went out for every meal. "Even breakfast?" she'd asked, and he'd nodded.

This morning, they were eating in a restaurant off Park Avenue, a place Kate was rapidly warming to. It was decorated like a 1940s diner, with a real, old-fashioned soda fountain, a black and white tiled floor and with booth seating in pale blue leather. After the first morning, Kate had realised she should only order a child's size portion of scrambled eggs and toast, as the adult one was alarmingly massive.

As they ate, she looked across at Tin. In some ways, he was reassuringly the same as the man she'd kissed goodbye at the airport all those months ago. In others, he was developing something of a New York gloss, an aura of sophistication and glamour that very much wasn't what she was used to. Once or twice, she'd heard the tinge of an American accent in his voice. Perhaps it was just the slang he was beginning to pick up, but for a moment, it made her feel rather lost and lonely. Would she end up like that if she moved here?

After breakfast, Tin announced he would show her Central Park. It was quite a fine day, although cold, and they set off, hand in hand, for their destination.

"You know what's strange?" Kate asked, as they waited to cross Seventh Avenue.

"What's that?"

"It just all seems weirdly familiar. The streets and the buildings. It's almost as if I've been here before."

Tin laughed. "In a past life, maybe."

"No, it's not that," said Kate, seriously. "I think it's because in England, we see so much of New York on the TV, don't we, and in films and things. We grow up watching it. No wonder it looks familiar." She looked up as they passed the Algonquin Hotel. "I love all the art deco design."

"You want to go to Miami for that," said Tin, piloting her onto the pavement on the other side of 44th Street. "Damn it, I should have gone a different way, sorry. This is going to take a bit longer than I anticipated."

"That's fine," said Kate, quite happy to see a bit more of New York as they walked on.

Eventually, they reached one of the entrances to the park. The sun had disappeared behind a blanket of thick, grey cloud and Kate pulled the neck of her coat tighter.

"What's it like back in England?" asked Tin. "The weather, I mean."

"Just as it always is. Some rain, some sun and you never know what you're going to get."

"Yeah, I remember."

Kate stole a sideways glance at her boyfriend. "Do you – do you miss it?"

Tin glanced over at her. "I miss *you*. I can't say I particularly miss England. It seems – oh, it seems really small now. Even London."

"Oh." Kate was conscious of a small heart-sink moment. She realised then that she'd been half hoping that Tin would be so homesick that he'd decided to come back to the UK.

They walked on along the winding paths, past a children's playground where a small group of toddlers and pre-schoolers were climbing on the equipment and digging in the sandpit. Kate knew that this was as good a moment as any to ask what she wanted to ask, but she quailed just the same. Perhaps she should leave it for a better moment. *This is as good a moment as you're going to get.*

She took a deep breath. "Listen, Tin." She saw him turn to her, eyebrows raised and plunged on. "If – *if* I move out here, will we – will we get married?"

There. It was out. Tin stopped walking and dropped her hand.

"What?"

Kate drew in another breath and repeated herself. "Will we get married?"

Tin made a surprised face. "Well, I – do you want to?"

Kate opened her mouth to say a firm 'yes' and surprised herself by hedging at the last minute. "Well, I suppose – I think it would be a good idea."

"Oh." After a moment, Tin began walking again but he didn't take her hand. "Well, I – I hadn't really thought about it, to be honest. I hadn't really thought about getting married."

Kate was conscious of a surge of anger. Chloe's words rose up in her mind once more. *If you move out there, you're giving up your job, your house, your friends, your family, God knows what else, and for what? For a man who won't even make any kind of commitment to you?*

"Don't you think you're asking rather a lot of me to

give up everything in my life back home and come out here without any sort of promise of commitment?"

Tin looked astonished and then uneasy. "Well – I can sort of see that but – but there's no point in rushing into anything, is there? I mean, marriage – that's a huge deal, that's a huge commitment, right there."

The anger surged again. "But me giving up my entire *life* for you isn't a big deal?"

Now Tin was starting to frown too. "Hold on, I wasn't saying that. You're twisting my words—"

"No, I'm not."

"Kate – you took me a bit by surprise, that's all. I'm not saying 'no', I just need a bit of time to think about it, that's all."

"Well, you shouldn't," said Kate, surprising herself again. "You should know. By now, you should *know*."

"You can't ask that. You can't demand that."

They stared at each other, all good feeling having evaporated into the chilly air.

"You don't think I've at least got the right to know that the man who expects me to move countries for him is actually serious about me?" asked Kate. She could hear the anger in her voice. Once, she would have perhaps thought about moderating her tone, being more conciliatory, putting Tin's feelings first. Now, her overriding feeling was *sod it. If I can't talk honestly about how I'm feeling and what I want, then what's the point in any of this?*

She said as much. Tin, with lowered brows, shook

his head. "You're ruining what should be a nice day. Why do we have to talk about this *now*?"

"Well, when would be a good time to talk about it, then?" demanded Kate. "When I'm back home, thousands of miles away? Or how about never? I just pack up my life and move out here to live with a man who can't even have an honest conversation about where our relationship is going—"

"Oh, I've had enough of this." Tin raised a hand in dismissal and turned on his heel. "I'll talk to you when you've calmed down a bit," was his parting shot, delivered over his shoulder.

Teeth clenched, Kate watched him walk away. Compounding the anger was the thought that her boyfriend had just left her adrift and alone in the middle of a strange city. She wasn't even sure how to get back to his apartment from here. Kate blinked back furious tears and made her way over to a convenient park bench.

Staring at the ground in front of her, refusing to look up and try and see where Tin had got to, Kate thrust her cold hands into her jacket pockets and stiffened her jaw. She would *not* cry. Of all the things that pissed her off about being a woman, near the top of the list was her inability to get angry without getting upset at the same time. At least in personal situations. She seemed to manage it at work all right.

Next to the bench was a flowerbed, the sad remains of some brownish daffodils clumped together. Kate stared at them. Rising up inside her was the inescapable knowledge that this was it, with Tin. Really, this was *it*. She'd been fighting against the realisation for so long, for so many reasons. The fact that she was getting older. The fact she'd invested years in this relationship. The fact that she loved him and – she was still sure – he loved her. But not enough. Not enough to make that commitment that would have proved to Kate that he had her back, that he was in it for the long haul.

*

IT WAS THERE, SITTING ON a cold bench in Central Park, looking at some dead flowers, that Kate realised she was never going to move to New York. All her life was at home in Abbeyford. She was never going to give that up. And Tin didn't love her enough to move back to England. That wasn't a crime. Even in the depths of her despair, she could at least be fair to him. They wanted different things, that was all. They'd met at the wrong time, or perhaps, deep down, they really weren't the right people for one another.

Damn and blast it, the tears were coming anyway, despite her best efforts. Kate fished for a tissue in her pocket and bent forward, hiding her face. She'd never felt further away from home or lonelier than she did at that moment. She wished fervently that she could teleport herself home, onto the sofa in her house, Merlin ready and waiting to jump into her lap. But no matter how hard she wished, that was never going to happen, was it? That was being an adult, wasn't it? Wading your way through all the crap life throws at you because that's just what you had to do, whether you wanted to or not.

There was the scuff of a footstep in front of her and Kate raised her head to see Tin standing in front of her, looking sad and tired.

"Come on," was all he said. "I've had enough of walking."

Kate heaved herself up. She felt as if she'd been up for more than a day already. "Me too."

Tin began to walk away. Kate followed him, only stopping to bend down and snap off the shrivelled brown head of a dead daffodil to put in her pocket, before she set off after her now ex-boyfriend.

Chapter Seventeen

"KATE!" OLBECK CRIED, ALMOST RUNNING from his office to throw his arms around her as she wearily divested herself of her jacket at her desk. "You're back! How was Tin? How was the Big Apple?"

Kate had been smiling, genuinely pleased at the warmth of her friend's welcome. Now the smile dropped off her face. "That's another story for another day. Can we leave it for now? I'm glad to be back, let's just say."

"Oh. Oh, right." Olbeck drooped a little "Sure. Sure. It's not the time, anyway. We've got too much work stuff to catch up on."

Kate groaned, slightly deceitfully as she'd felt a pure spasm of joy at the thought of getting back into the thick of it. "Let me grab a coffee and we can catch up, if you've got the time?" She sometimes had to remind herself that, as a more senior officer, Olbeck's hours were slightly more circumscribed than hers.

"That's fine, I'm good for the next half hour. Come on over once you're ready."

Chloe had clearly been listening in on this exchange with half an ear. She looked up, as Olbeck walked away, and caught Kate's eye.

"Don't—" warned Kate, worried that if anyone gave her the slightest sympathy, that she might burst into tears.

"Wasn't going to say a word." Chloe dropped her gaze and then raised it again to wink. "Glad you're back. Bird."

Kate gave a wan smile. "I'm glad to be back. Bird." She dropped into her chair with a sigh. "So, anything I should know about?"

"Mark will probably go through it all with you but there's one big development—"

"Yes?"

Chloe smiled grimly. "Melanie Houghton's been arrested. The house search turned up a raincoat just like the one worn by our mystery woman in the CCTV video."

Kate found herself making an 'ooh' noise. "You don't say."

"I do say. Theo and Anderton are questioning her now."

"Right," said Kate, mind going a million miles an hour as she pondered the possibilities. She saw Olbeck waving to her from his desk behind his glass office wall. "Thanks. We'll catch up later."

"Sure."

Kate hurried to the kitchen area, slopped some hot

water onto a hastily spooned mess of coffee granules and then hurried back to Olbeck's office.

"What's all this about Melanie Houghton being arrested?"

Olbeck grinned. "Well. It's like this. Melanie Houghton's been arrested."

Kate rolled her eyes. "Presumably on – well, on what grounds? Finding a bloody raincoat?"

"Do I detect a touch of cynicism in your dulcet tones, Kate? Yes, the raincoat. Plus, we've pulled her phone records and gone through them with a fine-tooth comb. She's had contact with our murder victim for months. One of Simon Farraday's other squeezes confirmed that he told them about the secret entrance to the townhouse, so there's no reason to suppose that Melanie Houghton wouldn't have known about it and used it. Like on the night of the murder."

Kate had been slowly sipping her muddy coffee through Olbeck's speech. Grimacing, she put it down and leant forward. "Trouble is, though, if that's Melanie Houghton on the tape, why come in through the front door? Especially if you're going to commit a murder? Why wouldn't you stay out of sight? It doesn't make sense."

"No," admitted Olbeck. "Perhaps Anderton can get something out of her on that little issue."

Kate drummed her fingers on his desk. "Do we have any tangible evidence that she knew about the tunnel? On a text message or something? An email?"

Olbeck shook his head reluctantly. "No, unfortunately. From the evidence of Simon Farraday's other lover, it was something that came into everyday conversation. Pillow talk."

Kate blew out her cheeks and sat back. "I suppose it comes down to proving that's Melanie Houghton on the CCTV."

"Ah, now, hopefully that's something that *is* going right. Anderton's had the footage sent off to a specialist, to see if we can get any more clarity on who it actually is." Olbeck sat back in his chair and spread his hands. "Hopefully we might have that in a week or so."

Kate got up and began pacing back and forth, trying to think things out. "Well, hopefully, by that time Melanie Houghton might have confessed." She stopped for a moment, punching her hand into her palm in frustration. "Where's the motive though? Why kill him – like that?"

Olbeck shrugged. "They were into that sort of thing. Bondage, domination. Suppose – suppose she just got carried away?"

Kate shook her head impatiently. "I've never heard of any kind of bondage that involves battering your lover over the head with a candlestick."

"Well, no, but you're not exactly on the scene, are you, Kate?" They looked at one another, Kate smiling reluctantly. "Supposing they were trying out some kind of role play and Melanie just lets rip, bangs him over the head and then realises what she's done?"

Kate stopped walking and turned to look at Olbeck. "What, it was just – just a moment of madness?"

"It's possible? Isn't it? You can imagine a man like Simon Farraday saying to his lover in the heat of the moment 'go on, hit me, hit me', probably not meaning, you know, on the *head* with a heavy metal object, but she mishears him or goes crazy or something like that, bashes him with the candlestick and then she's faced with what she's done."

Kate sat back down abruptly, staring at Olbeck. "You know, that *would* explain the CCTV."

"How do you mean?"

"Well, Melanie goes to the house all above board – well, not exactly *that*, but she's not trying to hide herself. In fact, she probably might not even realise there is CCTV in the square. But afterwards, after he's dead, she realises she has to get out without being seen. So she takes the secret exit."

They looked at one another, weighing up the possibilities. "That's a theory," said Olbeck. "I might just go and pass that on to Anderton. No – it's your idea. You do it."

"You sure?" Kate asked casually, hiding the not entirely unwelcome leap of excitement at the thought of seeing her boss again.

"Sure. I think they're in Interview Room Two." Kate threw him a grateful smile and got up. "Oh, and

Kate," said Olbeck, just as she was leaving his office. She turned back around enquiringly. "If you fancy dinner this week—"

"Oh—"

"Just an idea," said Olbeck. He smiled kindly. "Just – you know. If you want to talk."

"Thanks," Kate said, steadily. "I'll think about it. Thanks."

*

AS SHE MADE FOR THE stairs and the interview rooms, there was an unwelcome interlude of quietness that allowed her to start thinking again. Since she'd walked into the office, apart from that one wobbly moment when Olbeck and Chloe had greeted her, Kate had quite successfully managed not to think about Tin and the collapse of her relationship all morning. The moment her attention was distracted from the case, all those negative emotions came crashing back. *Don't think about it. Keep your mind on work.* She blinked furiously, pinched the side of her hand to regain her focus, and squared her shoulders before knocking on the door of Interview Room Two.

Anderton was too experienced an interviewer to look surprised when Kate popped her head around the door, but there was a momentary flicker on his face that Kate interpreted as pleasure in seeing her. "Yes, DS Redman?" he asked.

"Could I have a quick word, sir?"

Once outside and out of earshot of the two people remaining in the interview room, Anderton dropped the professional act. "Good to have you back, Kate." There was a moment when he feinted forward, almost as though he were going to hug her and Kate tensed, half willing, half reluctant. But he clearly thought better of it and converted the movement into a more fatherly pat on the shoulder. "How was New York?"

"Fine, thanks." Kate was perfecting the rictus smile that graced her face whenever anyone asked that question. "Anyway, I don't have time for that now. I wanted to talk to you about Melanie Houghton."

Anderton threw a glance back to the closed door of the interview room. "I'm making some progress. I think she thinks she's not got a lot to lose by telling the truth now."

"Really?" Kate was momentarily distracted. "Well, anyway, Mark and I came up with a theory that might explain the CCTV issue. Listen—" She carefully laid out the idea of Melanie Houghton losing control in the middle of a sex game, watching Anderton's face for his reaction.

He didn't look sceptical but he didn't look entirely convinced, either. "Mm. I suppose it's a possibility. She doesn't strike me as that type though but – well, I suppose it can't do any harm to see what she says." A thought seemed to strike him. "Are you busy now? Why don't you sit in?"

Kate *was* busy – five days off would do that to

a person – but after a moment's consideration, she decided to take Anderton up on his offer. She followed him back into the room and he started the interview again.

Kate sat silently, observing Melanie Houghton who was sitting opposite, next to a solicitor whom Kate didn't recognise. The man looked rather startlingly like Anderton; urbane, grey-haired, fifty-something. He could have been Anderton's cousin, perhaps even a brother. Kate wondered whether Anderton had noticed the resemblance but thought he'd probably been concentrating more on his suspect than her legal representative.

Melanie Houghton no longer looked ill. Instead she looked angry. She sat very upright in her uncomfortable chair, her eyes snapping sparks.

"I'm sorry about that, Mrs Houghton," Anderton said pleasantly as he sat back down again. "My colleague needed to speak to me. Now, we were talking about your relationship with Mr Farraday, weren't we?"

"You were questioning me about our affair, yes." Melanie spoke as if her jaws were clenched.

"You still maintain that you did not meet Mr Faraday on the night of the ninth of April?"

"As I have said, numerous times, I did not. We did not arrange to meet, we did not meet. I don't know how many times you keep wanting me to say the same thing." The Anderton-clone solicitor shifted uneasily beside his client, but Melanie took no notice. She folded her arms and stared across the table defiantly.

Anderton looked ostentatiously down at the folder he held on his lap. "We have a woman resembling you, wearing a coat very like the one we found at your house, entering the townhouse of Simon Farraday just before he was murdered."

Melanie interrupted him. "That was not me."

Anderton took no notice. "There is DNA evidence linking you to the scene."

"I can't help that. I have quite openly said that I used to meet Simon at the house all the time. Of course my DNA will be there. I was not there when he was killed." Her face flickered for a moment when she uttered those last words. Kate watched closely, trying to ascertain the emotion. Guilt? Grief?

Anderton cleared his throat. "There are messages on the 4Adults website between the two of you, back and forth between your two accounts, arranging to meet up on the night of the murder."

Melanie stared, stonily. "I did not send those messages."

Kate felt rather than heard Anderton's tiny sigh. He shifted position slightly and his leg touched Kate's. She was suddenly very aware of its warmth beneath the table and felt her heart begin to beat a little faster. What was wrong with her? Keep your mind on the job, she told herself, not for the first time that morning.

Anderton leant forward, going in for the kill. "You

and Mr Farraday enjoyed – if that's the right word – a fully sadomasochistic sexual relationship, didn't you, Mrs Houghton?"

"That's not against the law," Melanie said coldly.

"Yes, I know that. But killing people *is* against the law, Mrs Houghton. Did you get carried away on the night of the ninth of April? Did you hit Simon Farraday over the head?"

"I did not." Melanie folded her arms and leant back in her seat.

"Did you forget your safe word? Is that what happened?"

"I—"Melanie began but her lawyer spoke across her, saying her name in a warning tone. She gave him a sulky glance and said "No – no comment."

Kate sighed inwardly. They'd reached the stonewall stage of the interview.

"Did you lose control and kill Simon Farraday?" Anderton persisted.

"No comment."

Kate knew one thing that might break this conversational deadlock – a change of questions. She pressed her foot against Anderton's under the table – their old signal. He sat back, nodding at her very slightly.

"Where was this relationship going, Mrs Houghton?" Kate asked, deliberately cultivating a mild tone.

Melanie was obviously thrown by the change of interviewer, subject and pace. "What?"

"I just wondered where your relationship with Mr Farraday was going? You'd been seeing him for six months or so, so obviously it was quite serious. You – you loved each other?"

Melanie Houghton stared at Kate as if she'd never seen her before. "Yes. Yes, we did," she said, after a moment. Again, Kate saw that flicker of emotion on her face.

"You must be feeling pretty devastated right now," said Kate, putting as much sympathy in her voice as she could. It worked – she could see tears gathering in Melanie Houghton's eyes.

"Yes. I am."

Kate opened her mouth to say something else, but Melanie hadn't finished speaking. In a voice roughened with tears, she said, "Well, actually, we were very serious. I wasn't going to say anything about this because – well, I just wasn't—" Her solicitor twitched but she ignored it. "But I don't see any point in keeping it a secret any longer. Simon and I, we were – well, we were going to be together. Permanently."

A moment's silence. Melanie Houghton must have interpreted it as disbelief, because she flushed angrily and said, "It's true. We were going to leave our – our partners and be together. So now that you know that, why should you think I wanted to kill him? Or that I did kill him? I loved him, and he loved me. We were going to be together."

Chapter Eighteen

"So *she* says," said Anderton, seating himself behind his desk. Kate hovered by the doorway.

"You don't believe her?" Kate asked.

"I'm not sure I believe a word that woman says. She's – she's a funny one. Comes across as so self-righteous and proper and yet..." He let the sentence trail away. "Besides, even she can't argue that we don't have a case against her."

"I know." Kate sat down, feeling that this was going to be more than a five-minute conversation. "It's just that there's too many holes in it at the moment."

"You think I don't know that? I tell you, slap this little lot before the CPS and they'll laugh us out of the room. No, I need more evidence. I need a real motive." He churned his hair for a moment, obviously thinking. "Kate, do a bit of background for me, would you? Go and talk to a few people who knew Simon Farraday. Do some digging on the kind of man he was."

"I will," said Kate, slowly. "I've been thinking – I

wonder whether this has got anything to do with something that happened in the past. In his past."

Anderton eyed her. "What do you mean?"

Kate sighed. "I'm not sure. It's just – I get the feeling that this murder was either completely spontaneous or it's been very carefully planned. In fact, I think it's been very carefully planned so it *looks* spontaneous." She saw Anderton watching her and hurriedly added, "I can't tell you why that is at the moment. It's just a feeling I have."

"I know you and your feelings," Anderton said, but he was smiling. "Anyway, if you can do a bit more research for me on Simon Farraday, past and present, I think that would help."

"Of course." Kate got up and smiled at her boss. "I'll make a start straight away."

*

BACK AT HER DESK, SHE found the appropriate folder and began to flick through the paperwork within it, noting down several names. Interview Dorothy Smelton, perhaps? That would be a good starting point. Councillor Smelton had known Simon Farraday and was a friend of his wife's. Kate wrote down her name, adding Ewan Askell's and, after a small hesitation, the name of the Farradays' nanny, Sarah Collins. Hadn't both Kate and Olbeck thought that she had been concealing something? Now knowing something of the dead man's character, Kate was grimly certain that she had a pretty good idea of what the nanny's secret was. But she could be wrong... Only one way to find out. Kate made some phone calls, picked up her bag and prepared to leave.

"You all right?" Chloe asked, quite casually.

"I'm fine," Kate said, not meeting her eye. Then she relented. "No, I'm not fine, really. But I don't particularly want to discuss it right now, okay?"

"Okay, okay," said Chloe, hurriedly. "But I'm always on the end of the phone, if that helps."

"Thanks. Look, I've got to go. Talk to you later—"

"Where are you off to?" asked Chloe, professional interest clearly edging out personal concern. Despite her misery, Kate hid a grin. She and Chloe were two of a kind.

"Chasing up the dirt on Simon Farraday."

"No doubt there will be plenty of that."

"Yes." Kate hesitated and said "Actually, you know what? I think he might have had an affair with the nanny. Or slept with her, at least."

Chloe wrinkled her neat nose. "God, what *is* it with all this shagging? He wasn't *that* good looking."

"I don't know for certain," Kate said, honesty driving her to qualify her statement. "But I've got an inkling that's what she's hiding."

"You're probably right. Ugh, what an arsehole. Seriously, what did all these women see in him?"

Kate shouldered her bag. "He was confident, I suppose. Sure of getting what he wanted."

"Mm." Chloe busied herself with an email for a moment. After a minute, she looked up to find her colleague still standing in the same position, looking into space. "Kate? Earth to Kate? What's up?"

Kate came back to reality with a start. "Oh, nothing. It's just – something's given me an idea. Well, sort of. Something to look into, anyway."

"Right." Chloe was clearly waiting for her to elaborate, but Kate didn't. Instead, she waved at her colleague and said goodbye. Grabbing a pen and notebook from her desk as she left the room, she scribbled down one word on a piece of paper and then tucked it into her bag to use as a reminder later.

*

DOROTHY SMELTON WAS A RATHER masculine looking lady, considerably older than Kate had anticipated, given her friendship with thirty-something Mia Farraday. Her house was beautiful; an edifice of golden stone surrounded by verdant gardens. The sun shone brightly as Kate parked her car alongside Dorothy Smelton's enormous battered-looking Land Rover. Given the house and the car, and Dorothy's tweedy country demeanour, Kate was expecting a slobbery welcome from a big, hairy dog. A Labrador or perhaps a spaniel. But it seemed that Dorothy's dog had not long gone to the great kennel in the sky.

"Poor chap, he was in terrible pain at the end. I

always think it's rather odd, DS Redman, that we can happily end the suffering of our pets but we can't do the same for ourselves. Priorities seem somewhat skewed, don't they, in that regard?"

Kate agreed as she was shown through a lofty entrance hall, into a chintzy drawing room. Dorothy subsided onto an overstuffed Chesterfield sofa with an audible sigh. "Oh, bother, I forgot to ask if you wanted tea. Do you want tea?"

Kate declined politely, taking in her surroundings as discreetly as possible. Dorothy's home was both messy and far from clean but it had a cosy sort of feel, and beneath the clutter and detritus littering the floor and the furniture, the elegant structure of the house itself still made its presence felt.

"Now, Councillor Smelton, I understand that you've known Mia Farraday for some time?"

Dorothy was looking across to the window. "Sorry, did I ask if you wanted tea?"

"You did, thanks, Councillor, and I said no." Kate bit back a smile, remembering what Rav had said about the lady and her posh ways.

"I thought I had." Dorothy heaved herself into a more upright position and focused on Kate. She had gentle, faded blue eyes and her hair was stiffly combed and sprayed into an unflattering helmet, rather like the style Margaret Thatcher had worn as Prime Minister. "Yes, I *thought* I had. Silly me. Anyway, what was that? Mia? Lovely girl. Yes, I've known her for years. Her and Simon, God rest his soul. What a horrible thing that was." She leant forward a little and directed a question at Kate in what was almost a bark. "Got anyone for that yet, have you?"

"Not yet, Councillor, but we're definitely making progress. That's where I hope you can help me."

"Humph. Well, I'll do my best. Not sure what *I* can tell you."

Kate looked down at her list of questions and, on impulse, decided to ignore them for now. "I was hoping to talk to someone who could tell me a bit more about, well, Simon himself. What was he like? What was – what was his marriage like?" She could see Dorothy Smelton beginning to frown and hurried on. "It sounds prurient, I know, but sometimes it's the best way to build up a profile of the victim and who he – or she – knew. It can really help us to – to eliminate people."

"Humph." Dorothy Smelton was silent for so long that Kate wondered whether she should repeat the question. Finally, she said, quite abruptly, "Simon was a bad lot. That's all, really. Oh, don't get me wrong, he was charming. Too charming. Clever, hardworking, all that. Doesn't really mean anything when it comes to ethics. When it comes to morality."

Kate nodded. "Could you elaborate?" she asked, cautiously.

"Don't know if I can. He led Mia a merry dance, I know that. Treated her shamefully, with all his goings-on. Such a shame that all had to come out when he died. Would have been much better if he'd had a heart attack or something like that. A good deal less messy."

Again, Kate bit back an inappropriate smile. "Are you talking about his infidelity?"

"Am I? Yes, I suppose I am. Mia knew, of course. She's not stupid. Very clever girl, actually. Always felt she was a bit wasted on him." Dorothy sighed and shifted her bulk on the Chesterfield. "She was one of the brightest in her year at Edinburgh, and it's not that she told me that, you know. I knew one of her professors – ran into him not that long ago. I remember him saying exactly that to me. He was quite surprised when I told him she wasn't doing much else than being a wife and mother. Bit of a disappointment to him, I think. He mentioned that he thought Mia would have been a leader in her field by now. Not that I know much about that new-fangled stuff myself."

Kate was busy scribbling down notes. She nodded and asked "So, given that, you'd have said that the Farradays *weren't* particularly happily married?"

"I don't know about that." Dorothy's gaze strayed towards the window again. "Don't think they were particularly happy or unhappy. That's marriage for you, isn't it? Some ups, some downs..."

Kate found herself wondering whether the councillor herself had been married. She had been thinking of Dorothy Smelton as a lesbian, but perhaps she was just guilty of stereotyping. But then, did that explain the friendship between the two women, Mia and Dorothy? Or was Kate just being unbelievably crass and slightly homophobic? Surely two women could be friends without there being an underlying sexual motive? *I mean, look at me and Chloe...*

"Do you happen to know where Simon went to university?" she asked, bringing her mind back to the job.

"Not me. No idea." Dorothy was looking off into the middle distance. Kate wondered what she was thinking. The other woman added abruptly "Simon wasn't my friend, you know. We worked together on the council for a time. But no, we were never friends. Mia's my friend."

Kate smiled politely, thinking there wasn't much else to be gained from being here. "Thank you for your time, Councillor Smelton."

"You don't have to call me that. Call me Dorothy. *Should* call me Dorothy anyway, I'm retiring."

"Oh, I didn't realise that." Kate looked up from packing her things away in her handbag.

"Yes, retiring." Dorothy sunk her chin onto her chest, staring at the floor. "Time I did. Too tired for all that nonsense now. Getting a bit much for me."

Kate smiled politely, not entirely sure of what to say. Then she reiterated her thanks and took her leave.

Unlocking the car and taking a last, covetous look around the beautiful gardens, Kate found herself frowning. Something Dorothy Smelton had said had jarred, just a little. What had it been? For the life of her, Kate couldn't remember. She got into the driver's seat and looked through her notes of the interview, hoping that something would jump out at her. It didn't. What had Dorothy said? It was so little, so inconsequential, as tiny as a grain of sand. But, like a grain of sand in the wrong place, it irritated. Kate tried once more to remember what had been said and then gave up. From long experience, she knew that letting it go would mean it would come back to her. *Just give it time*. She turned her mind resolutely from whatever it was that had been bothering her, put the car into gear, and drove away.

Chapter Nineteen

EIGHT O'CLOCK THAT EVENING SAW Kate still in the office, bent over a pile of folders and her keyboard, a line of dirty coffee mugs on her desk testament to how long she'd been working. Gradually, the office had emptied out around her and now she was the only one remaining. She didn't mind. The thought of going home, even with Merlin there to greet her, filled her with dread. Too many empty rooms, too many silent thoughts to torment her...

The thought of her cat did make her pause, but the truth was that his feeding times had become so erratic while she was in New York that Kate was pretty certain he wouldn't be hungry for a good few hours yet. Perhaps not even until morning. No, she'd stay here as late as she could. She didn't feel tired at all – not physically tired, that is. Probably the jet lag to blame for that. Emotionally – well, she felt more as if she'd gone ten rounds with a heavyweight boxer.

"You still here?"

Anderton's voice made her jump. She swung

around in her chair to see him watching her from the doorway. "Afraid so. Just catching up."

"Come on, Kate, I'm not a slave driver. You must be exhausted. Why don't you go home?"

"I'm okay, thanks." Kate turned back to her desk and shuffled a few bits of paper around. Out of the corner of her eyes, she saw Anderton approach her.

"You all right?"

Kate had been dreading this question, especially from him. "I'm fine. Just tired." Too late, she realised she'd just contradicted herself. "I mean, I'm – I'll be done soon."

Anderton stood there for a moment, jingling his car keys in his hand. "Do you not want to go home?" he asked, after a few seconds.

How could he know? Kate found herself at a loss for words, mainly because her throat had suddenly closed up.

"All right," said Anderton. "How about a drink then?"

Of all the responses Kate had been expecting, that was not one of them. She stared at him for a moment, unable to answer. Then, without even thinking much of it, she said, "Yes. All right, then. Why not?"

*

AS THEY LEFT THE OFFICE together, Kate expected them to head towards the King's Head, the usual pub frequented by the officers of Abbeyford Station.

Instead, Anderton steered her towards the direction of his car. Surprised but, at that moment, too emotionally battered to think much more about it, Kate allowed herself to be shepherded into the passenger seat.

"Where are we going?" she enquired as they left the station car park.

"Little pub I know," Anderton said briefly.

"Oh."

"It does good food. I don't know about you but I'm starving."

Kate was hungry, in a distant sort of way, so she merely nodded. This was the first time she'd been alone with Anderton for a while – alone in a way that being alone with him in an office didn't resemble. She felt her heart beat a little faster. Inevitably, her thoughts turned to Tin, and she felt a jab of misery that immediately drove away any type of hunger pang.

"Here we are," Anderton said after about thirty minutes of silent driving. Kate looked around her. The pub was actually one she'd been to before with her boss, a lovely little country pub with a pretty beer garden, opposite a village green. She thrust the thought of how the hell she was going to get home from her mind and followed Anderton through the door of the pub. The lintel was so low he had to duck to get underneath it.

"Do you know why doors in old houses are so small?" Kate asked as they sat down at a small table at the back with their drinks.

"I have a feeling you're about to tell me."

Kate smiled a little sheepishly. "Well, it's not because everyone was tiny then. Although people were generally a bit smaller than they are now."

"So, what's the reason?"

"Doors were expensive. The bigger the door, the more it cost you. Hence most standard houses had pretty small doors." Kate took a sip of her drink.

"Well, you learn something new every day."

A not entirely uncomfortable silence fell over the table. Kate, casting around for a topic of conversation, was reminded of her upcoming interview with Ewan Askell. She said as much to Anderton. "I can't help wondering whether the fact that he's a bit of a history buff is significant. He must have known about that secret tunnel, mustn't he?"

Anderton took a pull at his pint. "You'll have to ask him. Didn't we find his DNA at the scene as well?"

"Well, technically not in the bedroom. We found several of his fingerprints in the kitchen area, and he did have an explanation for why they got there. Still—" Kate broke off, flipping a beer mat around and around on the table. "I don't know. He's got a motive."

"Which is?"

"Hating his former boss. Apparently, according to Mia Farraday, Simon treated him – Ewan – pretty badly. And that might not be all—" Again, Kate broke off, musing.

"Come on," said Anderton. "Spill the beans."

"I don't have any evidence. It's – it's more of a feeling. Mia Farraday did History at university. I wonder if there's more of a link between her and Ewan Askell than at first appears. I don't mean on Mia's side. As far as I can tell, she thinks of him just as a friend. Not even that – maybe a colleague. But when Ewan talks about her, I don't know..." Kate trailed off, the beer mat falling from her hand. "There's something there. What if he was in love with Mia – unrequited, I'm sure – and that gave him an added incentive to get rid of Simon?"

"That is pure conjecture," Anderton protested. "Come back to me with some evidence to prove it and I might start taking you seriously."

Kate smiled and shrugged. "I said it was only a theory."

Anderton had already finished his pint and started getting up to order another round.

"It's my round, isn't it?" asked Kate.

"Don't worry about that. My treat."

"Thanks." Kate watched as he went to the bar. That first glass of wine was already warming her stomach and beginning to relax her. She was suddenly very aware of the shape of Anderton's body, the long lean outline of him against the hard lines of the bar. Quickly, she looked away, back down to the smeary surface of the table.

Anderton put a fresh glass of wine in front of her. *I'd better be careful.* Kate was feeling too churned up to be able to act as she normally would. Alcohol probably wouldn't help.

She watched Anderton take a greedy mouthful of his fresh pint. "Are you driving home?" she asked, hoping she didn't sound quite as censorious as she thought she did.

Anderton looked surprised. "I'm walking home. I live just across the green over there."

"Oh." Kate hadn't realised he'd moved. But then, of course, he'd been divorced for several years now and his children were old enough to have moved out of the family home. She asked about them now.

"Oh fine, fine. Doing well at university. Costing me a fortune, of course."

Kate smiled dutifully. Silence fell once more.

"Well, I'll get us some menus," Anderton said eventually.

*

THEY ORDERED AND ATE AND spoke about work and the upcoming European referendum and about the bestselling book that Kate had finally managed to read on the flight home from New York (she had a thought as she spoke about it that the book would always be tainted by the memory of how she'd felt whilst reading it. She decided there and then it would be going to the charity shop at the earliest opportunity). They talked about Olbeck and whether he and Jeff would be successful in their hopes for adoption.

175

"Can't think of anyone who'd make a better father," Anderton said, and Kate agreed wholeheartedly. For a moment, she had a mad impulse to talk about her own experience with adoption, way back in her teens. It wasn't as if Anderton didn't know her history. He hadn't judged her. Or if he had, he'd hidden it very well. Kate realised, with an unpleasant jolt, that she'd never once told Tin of that little piece of her history. Not *once*, not even when Tin had confessed to her about his own little girl, Celeste, his daughter with a previous partner. Kate had never even met her. She stared down at her gravy-smeared plate, wondering why that was and why she hadn't thought fit to share with Tin that seminal event in her teens that had partly shaped her life. Was it because she had been afraid she would lose him over that particular revelation? Surely not? Or was it because, deep down, she hadn't been able to trust him?

Kate was so deep in thought that it took a moment for her to realise that Anderton was speaking to her.

"Sorry – I didn't hear you?"

"I said, I assume that you're not now going to be leaving us for New York?"

Startled, Kate jerked her head up. "What?"

Anderton regarded her over the rim of his pint glass. "You're not going to leave us and move to New York?"

"Oh." Kate let her head drop forward again. "No,

I'm not." She hoped her tone was neutral, but wasn't quite sure she'd been able to pull it off.

Anderton put down his pint glass. "Good," was all he said.

Kate began pulling the damp beer mat apart. "I'm not sure I ever thought I would," she said, almost to herself.

"I know."

That made her look up again. "You did?"

Anderton smiled. "Kate, you're an exceptional officer. You have some great friends here. Your family is here. What did New York actually have to offer you – apart from Tin?"

They stared at one another. Kate was the first to look away. "I'm sure you're right," she muttered.

"I'm sorry it didn't work out."

"Hmm."

Anderton put his empty glass on the table. "I'm not sorry you're staying. My God, I would miss you. *We* would miss you," he added, hastily.

Kate looked him in the eye. Something in her was tired of playing games. For the first time in her life, she didn't feel guilty or conflicted or worried about the situation here. Perhaps that was selfish of her. Perhaps it was just the wisdom that came with age. Perhaps if she'd listened to her heart when Tin had first told her he was leaving the country, she'd have broken it off with him there and then, avoiding months of uncertainty and misery.

For the first time in my life, I really know what I want, and I don't care whether I should have it or not. I just want it.

"I would miss *you*," she said, emphasising the last word.

They held each other's gaze over the table. There was a moment of hush, audible even over the noisy hubbub of the crowded pub. Kate held her breath. *Your move, Anderton.*

"Fancy a nightcap at my place?" he asked eventually, in quite a casual tone.

"Yes," said Kate, steadily, looking him in the eye. "Yes, I would."

Chapter Twenty

KATE HAD A MOMENT OF confusion when she woke the next morning. Her first thought, after she'd worked out where she was, was Merlin. He'd be hungry by now. She waited for the guilt to come flooding in – not just about Merlin, about the fact she'd slept with her boss *again* – but after a moment, she realised she wasn't feeling guilty. Not in the slightest. Instead she felt filled with exhilaration. She wasn't even embarrassed about being naked under Anderton's duvet.

She got up and found her way to the bathroom, where she located the towels in the airing cupboard and had a hot but brief shower. Wrapped in a navy blue bath sheet, she made her way back to the bedroom, where Anderton was still a buried shape beneath the bedclothes. He surfaced just as she quietly closed the bedroom door.

"God, you look indecently good in the mornings," he said. "Come here."

"I have to get going," Kate said, not meaning a word of it. But it felt so good to be able to tease a little...

"You're not going anywhere for at least – ooh, half an hour."

"Only half an hour?" said Kate, in mock outrage, but she walked towards the bed as she said it, loosening the towel as she got closer.

*

WELL OVER HALF AN HOUR later, Kate pulled on the final piece of her clothing and zipped up her boots. Anderton came back into the bedroom, now himself wrapped in a towel around his waist. Kate, who hadn't had so much sex in months, wondered briefly if she could pull him onto the bed for one last go before they left. Reluctantly, she dismissed the idea.

"Listen, I have to go straight to a meeting," said Anderton. "But I can drop you back at your place before that. Okay?"

"Fine. Thanks." Kate turned to her reflection in the mirror and attempted to smooth her bed-ravaged hair. Anderton came up behind her, nuzzled said hair to one side and kissed the back of her neck.

"Mm. Wish we didn't have to go."

"Well, we do," said Kate, her tone belying her body's reaction to his words.

"Yes, I suppose so." Anderton let her go. "It's probably best we don't drive into the office together anyway."

Kate immediately felt a drop in her stomach. "Why do you say that?"

Anderton caught her gaze in the mirror. "Oh, you

know what they're like, Kate. Total gossip-mongers. Let's not give them the satisfaction."

Kate stood up, feeling her heart start to thump. "Are you saying this was a mistake?"

"*No.*" Anderton's emphatic tone brought her a little comfort. "Not at all. My God, if it were up to me, I'd keep you here all day. No, all *week*. No, I just want – well – let's just see how things go, shall we? Without anyone else sticking their oar in."

Kate swung around to look at him properly. Half of her wanted to leap on the defensive, berate him for not giving her a straight answer or a declaration of undying love. The new, adult part of her turned over what he'd just said and decided he was right. "Okay."

Anderton looked relieved. He came closer, tipped her chin up with one hand and kissed her. "You really don't know how glad I am that you came back here last night," was all he said, but there was something heartfelt in his voice that at once both soothed and excited her.

"I'm glad too," was what she said. "But can you drop me back at the station car park anyway, because I need my car?" She thought for a moment and then said, with a grin "I'll wear some dark glasses if you think it'll help."

Anderton gave her a look which said quite a few things. "Come on," he said and slapped her bottom gently as she passed him in the doorway.

*

THEY TALKED ABOUT INCONSEQUENTIAL THINGS on the car journey. Kate was conscious of the fact of the police station drawing nearer and nearer and whether she would have the nerve to ask if they were going to see each other again. Obviously, they were going to see each other in *work,* but that wasn't the point... At length, Anderton drew in to the curb two streets away from the station and left the engine running. Kate was impressed to see he didn't even glance around to see if anyone was looking.

His goodbye kiss was long enough and passionate enough to soothe Kate's paranoia that this had just been another one-off. So did his parting words.

"I'm very much looking forward to when we can continue this," he said, after finally coming up for air.

Kate was so drenched in lust she found it difficult to speak. "Me too," she gasped, eventually.

Anderton gave her one final kiss. "See you later, then. I'll call you."

"Bye."

*

KATE KNEW SHE MUST HAVE driven home because somehow she found herself outside her house, but for the life of her she couldn't remember doing it, occupied as her mind had been with memories of what had just happened. She almost floated into the hallway and immediately tripped over Merlin, who was yowling as if he were being tortured. If the noise hadn't been much of a passion-killer, the scent of his unemptied litter box in the kitchen definitely was.

"Okay, okay, I'm sorry." Kate hastened to feed and water the frantic animal. "I'm really sorry for abandoning you."

She watched him eat his food without really seeing him, occupied as she was in replaying the night's events in her head. She and Anderton hadn't had a nightcap, of course. They'd barely got through the front door of his cottage before they'd started kissing. They hadn't even made it to the bed but had made love on the sofa in the living room, barely undressing. Kate shivered with remembered delight and then shrieked as Merlin leapt heavily onto her lap, obviously having forgiven her now his appetite was satiated.

Shouldn't you be thinking about Tin? The little guilt gremlin in Kate's mind was having a damn good try at being noticed again. Kate mentally pictured herself grabbing hold of it and hurling it out the window. *I am not going to feel guilty. I'm single, Anderton's single* (Is he? asked the gremlin, and Kate hastily swatted that thought) *and nobody's getting hurt.* She brushed aside the trifling fact that he was her boss and that she was still emotionally very vulnerable after a painful break-up. *I don't care.*

She tried to shake herself back into work mode. What was she supposed to be doing today? For a moment, her mind was a complete blank. Case? What case? *Get a hold of yourself, woman.*

Kate grabbed her phone and scrolled through her work emails, taking a quick look to see if she'd put anything in her calendar. Not interviewing Dorothy Smelton, she'd done that yesterday. Oh, yes, Ewan Askell, of course. She had an appointment with him at eleven thirty that morning. Kate took a look at the clock and gulped. She had approximately twenty minutes to drive to the Porthos offices which, for a journey of fifteen or so miles, really was pushing it a bit.

It was a beautiful spring day, warm, sunny and with the fresh new leaves on the trees beginning to deepen in colour. The hedgerows were foamy with the delicate white flowers of cow parsley, and the wheat fields were already filled with row upon row of sage green stalks. Kate hummed to herself as she drove along the country roads. Despite the ticking clock, she simply couldn't get worked up about being late. So what if she was? Did it really matter?

Her good mood saw her into the reception area of the Porthos building, where Ewan Askell was waiting for her. Breezy as she felt, Kate couldn't help but apologise for being ten minutes late, but her apology was brushed aside by Askell, who continued to smile anxiously as he showed her up to his office.

"Thank you for seeing me, Mr Askell." Kate seated herself opposite his desk, just as she had before. "I know you must be busy, particularly now you're holding the reins of the company."

"Well, yes—" Askell broke off, looking somewhat embarrassed. Kate found herself curious. What *would* happen to the company now that its founder and CEO had died? She asked the question as tactfully as she could.

"Oh, I'm sure we'll muddle on through." Askell had seated himself by this time and was fiddling with a pen, clicking the nib in and out. "We're having a meeting of the board of directors next week, and we'll no doubt plan out what's going to happen, both in the short term and the long term."

"Mrs Farraday will be attending that meeting, no doubt?" Kate asked, less because she was interested in the answer, more because she wanted to introduce the subject of Mia Farraday into the conversation.

"Yes, she should be there."

"It must be very hard for Mrs Farraday right now," Kate said, watching Askell's face closely. "She mentioned that you'd been to see her a week ago or so."

"Well I thought I had better pay my condolences," Askell said stiffly. "I wanted to see if she was all right, you know, given the circumstances."

"Yes, I can see that. I'm sure she appreciates the support of her friends." Kate paused, allowing the other man to interrupt her if he wanted to, with denials or agreement, but he said nothing. Kate wondered whether it was too early to ask what she wanted to ask but decided to go ahead. "I understand you and Mrs Farraday share something of an interest?"

Ewan Askell stared. "What do you mean?"

"You're both interested in history? Local history, perhaps?"

Askell continued to stare. "We are? I mean, I am, of course. I'm chair of my local history society. But as for it being one of Mia's hobbies, I'm not sure."

"You know Mrs Farraday studied History at university?"

"Did she?" Askell sounded only politely interested. "I didn't know that."

"She did. She also said that we could speak to you when we had questions about the Farradays' town house." Kate was still speaking when she felt again that jab of unease she'd felt just after interviewing Dorothy Smelton. Something had jarred, then, and it was jarring now. But what?

Askell was beginning to look a little alarmed. "Sorry, I don't understand. What is it that you wanted to know about the townhouse?"

Kate made an effort to dismiss whatever it was that was making her uneasy. "Oh, nothing much. You know, of course, about the secret entrance?" She half laughed. "That makes it sound very mysterious, doesn't it? I meant, about the tunnel from the cellar that leads out from the house."

Askell's face cleared. "Oh, *that*. Yes, yes I did know about that. Fascinating, isn't it? I remember Simon asking me about it once, what it really was, you know. I thought it might have been something to do with the

Reformation – the age of the house makes it likely – but it's really impossible to say for certain."

Kate, whilst listening politely, was aware of the total openness of his manner, the way he talked about the tunnel with no trace of self-consciousness or awareness of what his knowledge might mean in the context of the crime. Either he was an absolutely magnificent actor or he really was innocent of using the tunnel as a means of escape without detection from a murder.

Kate let him talk on a little more about the tunnel and then made an effort to steer the conversation back to the Farradays. "So, you've known the Farradays for some years, I understand. Do you think they were happily married?"

Askell, who'd relaxed considerably while talking about the tunnel in the townhouse, now stiffened again. "I'm sorry?"

"Do you think the Farradays were happily married?" As she repeated herself, Kate wondered whether she'd actually asked him that question before, in their previous interview.

His next words confirmed that she had. "You've asked me that, before, Detective Sergeant. My answer remains the same. They seemed happy enough to me."

Kate met his eye. "Really?" she asked, and she let her natural cynicism infuse the word.

Askell looked away. "Look, it's not my business to gossip. I don't know what you want me to say."

"I want the truth, Mr Askell. I'm sure you realise that the character of the victim can sometimes shed some illumination on the motive behind their murder. Don't you think that might be the case with Simon Farraday?"

She kept holding his gaze, wondering whether what she had just said was sinking in. After a moment, Askell sighed and sagged a little in his chair. "Look, Simon – Simon wasn't the easiest person to like," he said. He reached up and took off his silver spectacles, rubbing at the pink dent they had left either side of his nose. "He was brilliant, he was extremely driven, but he wasn't the easiest person to get on with."

"I gathered that," Kate said, drily but without too much emphasis. She wanted Askell to go on talking.

He did so, seeming to gain a little confidence as he went on. "Simon was also – oh, how shall I put it? He – he was a man of very large appetites."

"You mean women?"

Askell was too old to blush properly, but he looked uncomfortable. "Well, yes. That sort of thing."

"We know he had a lot of affairs, Mr Askell, if that's what you're talking about." For a moment, Kate wondered whether he was referring to some other sort of vice – drugs, perhaps. His next words reassured her.

"He had many affairs, that's true. He wasn't even particularly discreet about it, not once he knew I knew." Askell's face tightened. "I think he actually *enjoyed* me knowing. I don't think he minded anyone knowing, as long as they wouldn't take him up on it and make a fuss."

"Like his wife?"

Askell smiled unhappily. "Well, Mia's not stupid. I suppose she turned a blind eye for the sake of her family. It's not as if she had to run up against his lovers very often."

"*Very often*?"

Askell blinked at her emphatic tone. "Well, no. He mostly kept his – his affairs – to people he met through work, and Mia had very little to do with that side of his life, from what I could gather."

Through work or online. Kate found herself thinking about Sarah Collins, the Farradays' nanny, and the hesitation in her voice as she'd mentioned her male boss. She'd bet good money that Simon Farraday had slept with her too, walking male appendage that he'd been. *Disgusting old goat.* She found herself hoping quite fervently for a second that Mia Farraday would divorce him and take him to the proverbial cleaners, before coming back to reality and reminding herself that the randy old sod was already dead.

As if he'd read her mind, Askell mentioned something about it being easier for Mia now. "Of course, it's terrible for the children, and for her too, but I hope at least Simon's left all his affairs in order financially. He always kept a tight hold of the purse-strings."

"Oh yes?" Kate looked up from her notebook.

"Oh, I don't mean he was mean with money or anything like that. Quite the opposite. But he very much liked to be in control. In control of everything." Askell slipped his glasses back on and sighed. "I suppose that's what marriage used to be like, didn't it? The husband as the head of the family. Sounds a bit old-fashioned now, I suppose."

Suddenly, inspiration broke into Kate's mind in a shower of golden sparks. *That* was the phrase that had nagged her so much, the words that Dorothy Smelton had used that had niggled away at Kate without her being able to say exactly what they were. She almost gasped and then quickly collected herself.

"Mr Askell, thank you, you've been very helpful." There were in fact several questions she could have still asked him, but she wanted to get this little matter cleared up before doing anything further. "I might have to come back and see you again but what you've told me today has been very useful."

Askell didn't look as relieved as he might have done. Instead, he was looking rather sad. "It's funny," he said, "But just talking back over about Simon suddenly made me miss him, rather. I'd have said, just before you came, that I didn't miss him at all."

Kate smiled, rather distractedly. "These things take a long time to get over," she offered, packing up her bag.

"Yes, I suppose so. Well, do let me know if I can

be of any more help, DS Redman." He stood up to courteously show her from his office.

Kate said goodbye, shook hands, and then hurried to her car, anxious to go back through her notes before the sudden flash of inspiration disappeared. She flipped back through the pages of her notebook, searching for that one phrase that had caused her so much anxiety. There it was. Kate had actually jotted Dorothy Smelton's exact words down. Rather unusual for her to have done that. Perhaps her subconscious had been working well for her that day. Kate read it again. *Mia would have been a leader in her field by now. Not that I know much about that new-fangled stuff myself...*

Re-reading it, Kate frowned. It actually wasn't that much to go on, after all. Should she bother...? No, if she didn't find out exactly what Dorothy had meant by that, it would continue to nag her. She hauled her road map out from under the passenger seat, thinking that she was probably not too far from Dorothy Smelton's house here. She'd drop in on the way back to the station and find out, once and for all, what Dorothy had meant by that statement.

She tried to ring the landline – she had no mobile number for Dorothy Smelton – but there was no answer. Never mind, she'd just call in and hope that she would be home. Kate closed her notebook and put it back in her bag. Then she took one last look at the map, checking on her route, and drove away.

Chapter Twenty-One

DOROTHY SMELTON'S CAR WAS IN the driveway of her house when Kate pulled in through the gateway, which pleased her. Chances were Dorothy would be in. Kate parked the car, smoothed her hair down, and made her way to the front door.

Nobody answered her first ring of the ancient, clattering doorbell, nor the second. Kate hesitated, about to leave it and walk away, but a flicker in the glass of the door showed her that someone was actually in the house. She pressed the bell again for a third time and watched the flicker in the glass get nearer as the figure finally approached the door.

The door was yanked open with surprising speed, and Kate nearly jumped. Dorothy stood there on the doorstep peering suspiciously at her. "What is it?"

"Hello Councillor Smelton, it's me again, I'm afraid." Too late, Kate realised that Dorothy wasn't a councillor any longer. "May I have a few minutes?"

"Who?" Dorothy glared at her as if she suspected Kate of playing a practical joke.

"It's me, Detective Sergeant Redman—" Kate said, faltering a little at the look Dorothy gave her. "I was here yesterday, talking to you?"

Dorothy snorted, as if it was the most preposterous thing she'd ever heard. "Don't be ridiculous. Who are you? What do you want?"

Kate was beginning to have that dizzy feeling, the kind felt when the situation becomes oddly dreamlike. Was she going mad or was Dorothy?

"Dorothy, I'm Kate Redman, we met yesterday. We talked about Simon Farraday and his wife, your friend, Mia Farraday. Do you – do you not remember?"

"I don't know what you're talking about. You must think I was born yesterday, thinking you can just barge into the house. Go on, be off with you. Trying to trick me. Go on, off!"

The last word was accompanied by the slam of the front door, almost in Kate's face. She took a step back, shaken. What was going on? What *was* the matter with Dorothy?

She backed away from the house, troubled by what had just occurred. Did Dorothy truly not remember her? From a day ago? Or was she pretending not to know Kate for some other reason? But what?

Shaking her head, Kate returned to her car. She was half-inclined to try the door again but dismissed the idea. Dorothy wasn't under arrest – she wasn't even under suspicion. If she was pretending not to know Kate, for whatever strange reason of her own, then right at this moment, there wasn't anything much Kate could do about it. She'd just have to come back later and try again. Kate made a resolution to do just that. Whether or not she'd be more successful later was only half the point. She wanted to make sure Dorothy was okay.

She drove back to the office. The interview with Askell and the odd encounter with Dorothy Smelton had, for a while, driven thoughts of Tin and Anderton out of her head, but as she approached the station, she began once more to think about what had happened with her boss and whether it was going to be another big mistake or whether it might actually result in some sort of meaningful relationship this time.

Kate sat for a moment once she'd parked the car, collecting herself. She checked her appearance in the mirror. Not that it should matter but... Shaking her head at her reflection, she grabbed her bag and climbed out. Her nervousness at seeing Anderton again was growing. She had to take a moment to remind herself that she was a grown woman in her late thirties, not a teenage school girl about to come face to face with her crush.

As it happened, Anderton wasn't even in his office. Feeling a mixture of disappointment and relief, Kate headed for her desk.

"Afternoon, bird." Chloe gave her a greeting without even looking up. "Where have you been?"

Kate felt a secret satisfaction at how quickly she

was able to snap straight into work-mode. She flung her bag under her desk and sat down, reaching for her keyboard. "I've just come from Dorothy Smelton's house."

"Who?"

Kate explained what had happened. "You know, the councillor. Mia Farraday's friend. I went to see her to check something out, and she was really odd. *Really* odd. I'm wondering whether there might actually be something wrong with her."

"How do you mean?"

Kate stopped, thinking back on her strange encounter with Dorothy. "I'm not sure, exactly," she said, slowly. "It was like she didn't even recognise me."

"Are you sure that wasn't just her way of getting you to bugger off?"

"No," admitted Kate. "But I think I might pop in again later on, just to check she's okay."

"What was it that you wanted to ask her?"

"Well, that's just it." Kate retrieved her notebook and re-read the phrase that had so puzzled her. "Actually, I think I'll have a closer look at it myself. Perhaps I don't even need to speak to Mrs Smelton."

"What *are* you talking about, bird?"

Kate grinned. "Doesn't matter. *I* know what I mean."

"Well I'm glad somebody does."

Kate fetched them both a coffee and then sat down at her desk again. She wondered where to begin. It was such a tiny, insignificant remark. Was it even worth bothering with? She tapped a pencil on the edge of her jaw, her usual displacement activity when thinking. Then, making up her mind, she brought up the Google search bar and began to type.

She referred back to her notes, found the name of the institution she was looking for and carefully worked out the years in which she was interested. It took a while to track down the telephone number of the person she was looking for and at least three separate phone calls before she got through to their office. Then followed a lengthy rigmarole of Kate having to prove her identity by faxing through her identification and having the person she needed to speak to call her back through the police station reception desk.

She'd just put the phone down on them, their conversation having left her feeling more puzzled than ever, when Anderton appeared in the doorway to the office. Their eyes immediately met, and Kate felt her heart give a thump so painfully strong, she was surprised it wasn't audible to Chloe.

"Kate," Anderton called. "Have you got a minute?"

Thoughts of the phone call she'd just had fled in an instant. "Yes, I have – just one moment," Kate said as casually as she could. *Play it cool, play it cool...* Chloe obviously hadn't noticed anything amiss and wasn't even listening, intent as she was on her computer screen.

"Fine, just come and find me in my office," Anderton said, equally casually, turning away. Kate forced herself to wait two whole minutes, scribbling mindless doodles on her notepad, before getting up and making her way there.

The blinds were down in Anderton's office. Kate's heart rate increased to a pitch that almost made her feel nauseous. She knocked on the closed door – why was it closed? – wishing her hand was steadier.

"Hello," Anderton said as she closed the door behind her.

"Hello." The sight of him across the other side of the desk, dressed in his customary suit, and looking sternly professional, was so at odds with her memories of him from the night before that for a moment, Kate was convinced she'd dreamt the whole thing. This whole day was turning out to be somewhat dreamlike, she thought.

Then Anderton was getting up and approaching her and before she knew what was happening, was kissing her so deeply and at length, his arms around her, that for a moment she didn't know what to think or feel, or anything at all.

Eventually, he drew back. "Sorry," he said, a gasp in his voice. "But there's no way I could sit there and talk about work with you without doing that first."

Kate made a valiant effort to collect her scattered thoughts. "That's okay," she said, equally breathless.

"And, while we're on the subject, when are we going to see each other again?"

Kate felt like cheering. Cheering and crying. Outwardly, she smiled and said "Up to you."

"Well then, how about tomorrow night? Dinner?"

Kate had to struggle not to let her delight show too plainly. "I'd like that," she said, very proud of the even tone of her voice, that hopefully still conveyed to Anderton just how much she liked the idea.

"Good. Now—" There was a knock at the door, and Kate and Anderton sprang apart guiltily. Hastily, Kate took a seat, and Anderton hurried over to the window. "Come in?"

It was Olbeck. Kate was unprepared for the jab of guilt that hit her. Why did she feel guilty, when confronted with Olbeck's honest, open face and the smile he directed at her? She tried to smile back equally as enthusiastically.

"Mark!" Anderton cried, just a shade – Kate thought – too enthusiastically, but luckily Olbeck didn't appear to notice.

"I've just heard from the tape expert, you know the one looking at that CCTV footage. That one?" Anderton nodded and Olbeck continued. "Unfortunately, it's not great news. The tape quality is so bad that they weren't really able to get anything new from it. In fact, the guy said that he thought the camera itself was actually faulty and that's why the quality is so bad."

Kate watched Anderton himself switch into

work-mode and was secretly impressed. He was even better at it than she was. *Had more practice, probably*, said the little gremlin in her ear, and Kate tried not to grimace.

"That's a shame," Anderton said. "But it's not entirely unexpected. It was that same camera, wasn't it, that actually conked out completely later on that evening?"

"Yes, that's right. So unfortunately, this doesn't give us any more real evidence."

Anderton sighed. "*C'est la vie*, I suppose." He looked across at Kate. "Anyway, on we go. Was that everything you wanted Kate?"

There was nothing in his tone but Kate couldn't mistake the flirtatious look in his eyes. She frowned. It felt wrong to do this in front of Olbeck, innocent of the truth as he was. "Yes, that's all for now, thanks." She got up to go, not looking at him. Then, on her way to the door, something struck her. "By the way, where are we with Melanie Houghton?"

Anderton was too professional to look surprised but his eyebrows flickered minutely. "I'm still in two minds about charging her, but she's far and away our most likely suspect. She's on the scene, she arranged to meet our murder victim on the night of his death, she's been emotionally and sexually involved with him, she owns a raincoat very similar to the one seen by our CCTV suspect on the night of the murder, and her only alibi is from her husband." He sighed and added "The more I think about it, the more likely it seems that she's our girl."

Kate paused with her hand on the door to the office. Something that Anderton had said had chimed with her. "What about the motive?" she asked, slowly. "Didn't she say that they were in love, that he was planning to leave his wife for her? Why kill him?"

"I've been thinking about that," Olbeck said, unexpectedly. Both Kate and Anderton looked at him.

"Spill," was all Anderton said.

"Well, it's like this. What if it's all actually back to front? What if Simon Farraday confessed to her, right in the heat of the moment, that he *wasn't* going to leave his wife, that he didn't love her, or didn't love her enough to break up his family? What then? Is she consumed with jealousy, goes mad, hits him on the head?"

Both Kate and Anderton stared at him. "I suppose that's possible," was all Anderton said.

"It's only an idea," said Olbeck. "But you know we've been searching for motives since the start of this case. And I don't know about you, but I get the impression that this is a crime of passion, as it were. It's a murder taken place because of an emotional reaction."

Kate thought hard about what he'd just said. "I sort of know what you mean. But I get the impression that it's actually a calculated killing. Carefully planned to *look* like it's a crime of passion."

"So, it's murder for gain, then?" Olbeck looked

sceptical. "Who gains? Who gains that hasn't already been cleared?"

Anderton snorted. "Conjecture, conjecture, conjecture! I want *evidence*. Go on, both of you. Go out and get me some evidence before I hear one more word about motives or crimes of passion or dastardly plots."

He shooed them both out of his office and shut the door. Kate, inwardly smiling, was just thinking with delight about the night with him yet to come when Olbeck touched her arm. "Listen, are you okay?"

"I'm fine." Startled, Kate pulled herself together. "Just got a lot on my mind at the moment."

Olbeck looked sympathetic. "I know. It must be hard. Listen, we talked about dinner, didn't we? Could you do tomorrow?"

"No, sorry," Kate said, just a shade too quickly. Hurriedly, she qualified her statement. "I can't do *tomorrow* but it would be great to catch up soon. How about Friday?"

"That's a possibility. I'll check with Jeff." They began to walk back to the office. "Listen, what was that I heard you talking to Chloe about? Something about Dorothy Smelton?"

Dorothy Smelton was actually the furthest thing from Kate's mind at that moment. Jolted by the recollection of Dorothy's strange behaviour, she explained to Olbeck what had happened when she'd gone to see her that morning.

"Strange," said Olbeck with a frown. "I think you're right to go back and check on her."

"Yes," agreed Kate. "And in fact, that's what I'm going to do right now, on my way home."

Chapter Twenty-Two

ON HER WAY TO DOROTHY Smelton's house, Kate found herself easing her foot off the accelerator. There was a lay-by up ahead, and she pulled the car into it without thinking consciously of doing so. Then she turned the engine off and stared ahead through the windscreen.

It was a cool, grey evening, the sunshine of earlier hours long gone. Kate's driver side window was down, and she could hear the birds singing their songs as the twilight slowly gathered. Funny to think they were merely marking their territory. Not for the first time, Kate found herself wondering whether there really was a Higher Power. A bit like whenever she saw a rosebud, the absolute perfection contained in its curled petals. How could something that beautiful just evolve naturally?

Shaking off the philosophical thoughts, she took out her notebook and noted down all the points that were worrying her. *University course. Dorothy's behaviour. Check on house deeds? Motive – gain or emotion? Or both?*

Kate stared at what she'd written for a moment and then added *Jealousy*.

She re-read what she'd written again and then, very slowly, wrote *Trap?*

A final read-through, and then Kate, tutting in frustration, scribbled her pen all over the words she'd just written. There was something missing, a final thread that would pull all these disparate things together, but *what*? What *was* it? She fought the urge to hit her head against the steering wheel to try and knock the answer out of her stubborn brain.

Eventually, Kate sat up, started the car and pulled out of the lay-by. As she drove through the crumbling gateposts to Dorothy Smelton's driveway, she was suddenly aware of how tired she was. Had she and Anderton got *any* sleep last night? She found herself smiling, warm with remembered desire, and thinking ahead with anticipation to tomorrow night...

Nobody answered her ring on the doorbell. Kate, remembering what had happened earlier, tried again and again. Still nothing. She peered through the murky glass panes of the front door, trying to make out the inside of the house.

Stepping back, she yawned. Was it really worth continuing? Dorothy might very well be out, although – Kate glanced over at the car parked on the driveway – if she was, she must be on foot. She decided to have one last look around, and if she couldn't see sight nor sign of Dorothy, then she was going home.

She sighed and began to walk towards the front lawn, which wrapped around the house in a smooth green semi-circle. Although as Kate could see, as she got closer, it wasn't actually that smooth – in fact, the grass looked as though it hadn't been cut in some time. The flowerbeds, whilst a riot of colour, were also thick with weeds. Kate worked her way around the front of the house, peering in through the gap in the curtains, trying to see into the dim interior of the house. It was hopeless, like peering into a murky fish tank.

Stepping back, her foot connected with something hard and she looked down to see a blue and white pottery mug tipped over on its side. What was that doing in the flowerbed? Kate set it on the edge of the lawn and in doing so, spotted another, no more than one – was it *four*? Four mugs of different designs, scattered throughout the flowerbed. Frowning, she lined them all up at the edge of the lawn, wondering if Dorothy had left them there. Had she just forgotten them? All four?

The silent house was beginning to give her the creeps. Kate walked quickly around the perimeter, peering in at the windows, and gave thanks that this house wasn't overlooked by any neighbours. No doubt in a busy street, her suspicious behaviour would be reported to the police. How ironic...

She found the back door to the house, hidden

away under a little porch. Boxes of empty glass jars, bottles and tins were piled up untidily either side of it. A mouldering heap of old carpet was slung against the back wall. The actual house itself looked quite neglected, now that Kate took a closer look at it. The paint was peeling from the rotting window frames and the mortar between the golden stone slabs was crumbling away. Too big a house for one elderly lady on her own, Kate thought, having visited many similar looking properties with similar occupants.

She sighed again and began to walk back around to the front. She may as well go home. It was beginning to get dark now, and she was feeling very tired. Not to mention poor Merlin shouldn't go *another* night without his dinner being served at a reasonable time.

Kate made for the front door once more and tried the bell, just once more. She could hear it clattering away in the silent house. Nobody answered. Just on the off chance, she tried the front door handle and was surprised when it turned under her palm.

Kate stood there before the open door, wondering what to do. Should she go in? She cast a longing look back to her car, thinking of how much she'd like to go home right now, and then pushed the door open a little further.

"Councillor Smelton? Dorothy? Are you there?"

No answer. Kate stepped forward into the spectacularly untidy hallway. "Dorothy? Mrs Smelton? Are you there? It's me, Detective Sergeant Redman..."

A few steps into the hallway and Kate stopped. The silence pressed down upon her like a thick, grey blanket. She found herself holding her breath. She could see what had to be the kitchen at the end of the hallway, the edge of a table, a chair. She tried calling one more time, turned her head to look into the drawing room at the front of the house and gasped.

Dorothy Smelton lay half on and half off of the Chesterfield sofa, her face turned into the back of the chair, one arm hanging downwards, her fingers almost brushing the floor. As Kate ran forward, she heard a crunch as she dropped to her knees by the sofa and felt the disintegration of something small and round beneath her kneecap. She could see Dorothy was dead, just by the colour of her skin, her stillness, the vacancy that sucked at the air around her, but still Kate pressed her fingers against Dorothy's neck. No pulse beat beneath her hand and she could feel what little residual warmth that remained in the body ebbing away.

Slowly, because she was shaking a little, Kate got up and brushed away the crushed pill that had stuck to her knees. Looking around, she could see more pills scattered all about the sofa. A half empty bottle of brandy or whisky, some sort of brown spirit, stood a little way away, with an overturned glass beside it. Kate looked for a note but there was nothing she could see. She tried to recall what Dorothy had been wearing earlier that day, when she'd chased Kate off her property. It was hopeless; she couldn't recall a thing. Was that why Dorothy had pretended not to know her? Because she'd decided to kill herself and didn't want anyone stopping her?

Taking a few deep breaths, her head swimming from the brandy fumes rising from the carpet, Kate knew she could do nothing more for poor Dorothy now. Nothing except one thing. She dialled Anderton's number and waited for him to answer, thoughts of a romantic nature utterly forgotten.

*

FIVE HOURS LATER, THE POWERFUL arc lights of the Scene of Crime Team dyed the walls of Dorothy Smelton's living room blue-white. The unforgiving light showed all of the disorder in which Dorothy had obviously been living. The high ceilings were webbed with thick ropes of grey cobweb and dust, fluff and other assorted minuscule scraps lay in clumpy heaps by the skirting board.

Kate stood over to the side of the room, with Anderton at her side and Olbeck on the other. They hadn't said much on meeting, and Kate was glad that Anderton had made no attempt to give her so much as a meaningful glance. Not that he could have done that in front of Olbeck but... Kate hoped he wouldn't try to murmur something in her ear or even touch her. It just wouldn't be appropriate, not in this sad setting.

He showed no signs of doing anything like that,

though. Instead, he'd shaken his head on first seeing Dorothy's body, which was now being examined by Andrew Stanton.

"No note, I suppose?" he'd asked Kate on arrival.

"Not that I could see. I haven't had a really good look around, though."

Anderton glanced around him in distaste. "Well, you'd have your work cut out here."

Now, Olbeck bestirred himself and said "They don't always leave a note, do they?"

Anderton shook his head again. "No. Half the time they don't." He sighed and said "Well, it's likely we don't even need to be here." He looked as if he were about to shout a question to Dr Stanton but obviously thought better of it. Andrew Stanton could be quite tetchy if interrupted at the wrong time. "Suppose we'd better have a look around while we're here and waiting."

*

THE THREE OF THEM WERE already suited and gloved, as was standard procedure for a potential crime scene. Kate decided she would tackle the upstairs rooms, leaving the two men to look downstairs. She felt it wise to be far away from Anderton at that point in time. There was no point putting temptation in either of their ways.

The stairs in Dorothy's house were wide, with a shallow tread, a carved wooden banister running up one side, a filthy carpet runner cascading down the middle. Kate climbed, feeling rather depressed. Suicides always filled her with a horrible sense of emptiness. It was hard to contemplate, the fact of someone's unhappiness being so great that the only way they could see to escape it was to kill themselves. Was that why Dorothy had been so odd when Kate had seen her earlier? Could that really only have been this morning? It seemed like a week ago. Kate yawned, wondering how long they would have to remain here. If it was a genuine suicide – and why wouldn't it be? – it wouldn't be the team's problem.

Kate stopped at the entrance to what was clearly Dorothy's bedroom, frowning. She'd just had a thought, but it had been so brief and so quick that now she couldn't recall what it was. I'm just too tired, she thought, yawning again, and went into the room.

It had probably once been a very lovely room, country-charming, with the walls papered in a floral pattern; tiny sprigs of white roses intertwined with bluebells, pale silver stripes running down between the flowers from floor to ceiling. The little dormer window showed a vista of varying shades of green; hills and valleys and the tiny glittering thread of the river Avon in the distance. But the room itself was cluttered and filthy, the wooden floors scuffed and stained, marked and dust-strewn. The wallpaper around the light switch by the door was black with grease. The yellowing bedclothes looked as though they hadn't been changed in a month.

Kate stood, wrinkling her nose and trying not to judge. Had Dorothy been ill? Or was she just elderly and forgetful, and housekeeping was one of those things that had slipped? *She's just killed herself, woman.* If Dorothy had suffered from depression, all this mess and disorder was entirely understandable.

Kate headed for the little bathroom, which was in a similar state to the bedroom. Forcing open the rusty catch of the little bathroom window, Kate took a deep, grateful gulp of the night air flowing in through the gap between wall and window. There was a little medicine cabinet above the dirty sink and Kate opened it cautiously. There were a plethora of medicine bottles and packets all jumbled together on the narrow shelves. Kate recognised some of the brand names but not the others. She checked her gloves were on properly and took up a couple to read the labels.

Donepezil. Kate read it again. It meant nothing to her. She read another, this time recognising a brand of anti-depressants. That bottle looked new and unopened. Pondering, she picked up the bottle of Donepezil and took it downstairs.

Andrew Stanton was just zipping up his black bag. Kate took a quick look at Dorothy's body. It was strange, but there was a moment after death – and it varied from corpse to corpse – where for a short time the person really did look as though they could be sleeping. As if a touch would wake them. If the death had been relatively peaceful of course, Kate corrected herself. But then there came a point where the illusion no longer stood. The dead became truly dead. The person who'd once inhabited that body was gone, indisputably gone, and that had happened to Dorothy now. Kate, looking at her dead face, knew she wasn't there anymore.

"Andrew—"

"Oh, hi, Kate. I didn't even realise you were here."

"I've been upstairs. I found these in the bathroom cabinet." Out of the corner of her eye, Kate saw Anderton and Olbeck enter the room, both empty-handed and looking tired. "Do you know what it is?"

Andrew glanced at the little brown bottle Kate was holding out. "Donepezil? Sure. It's a cholinesterase inhibitor."

Kate gave him a look. "Which means?"

"Oh, it's used in the treatment of Alzheimer's. Sorry, that's a bit of a misnomer, it's not a *treatment*. There isn't such a thing, unfortunately. But it's given to sufferers to help relieve some of the symptoms."

Kate looked again at Dorothy's dead face. "She had Alzheimer's?"

"I don't know. I can't tell from a preliminary investigation. We'll have a better idea at the PM." Andrew threw an eloquent look at the chaos surrounding them. "Judging by the state of this place, it's not beyond the realms of possibility, is it?"

The other two officers had reached them by now. All four of them took another look at the dead body on the sofa, more neatly arranged by Andrew Stanton.

"I suppose that's as good as a note," Olbeck said sadly.

No one contradicted him. Instead, they stood in a little bubble of silence, busy with their own thoughts, as the bustle and hubbub of the investigation went on around them.

Chapter Twenty-Three

KATE SLEPT DEEPLY THAT NIGHT, untroubled by dreams of Dorothy or Tin or Anderton. She awoke to her curtains outlined in bright sunlight and the warmth of Merlin draped over the hump of her feet under the covers. Kate blinked herself awake, wondering why she was feeling an uneasy mix of anticipation and foreboding.

The anticipation was easy to track down. Hadn't Anderton said something about going out for dinner tonight? Kate smiled to herself. Was this actually going to turn into a relationship? Should it? Could it? Thoughts of Tin tried to muscle their way in, but it was easy to dismiss them. Perhaps it was wrong, but the memory of her ex-boyfriend seemed to be fading into sepia – black and white, even – while the corporeal reality of Anderton stood out in blazing technicolour.

Kate got up and began her morning routine: shower, hair-wash, wrapped in her new White Company robe (a present to herself in an attempt to cheer herself up after things fell apart with Tin. You couldn't go far wrong with some luxurious new nightwear, in Kate's opinion). She went downstairs, fed a noisily mewing Merlin, and sat down to eat her breakfast.

The anticipation of the evening to come dimmed as the sense of foreboding grew. What was wrong? The itch of a nagging, unfocused thought was back again, scratching at her brain. Kate downed the last of her coffee and tried to collect herself.

It was a beautiful morning, the sky a cool, clear blue, the sun shining brightly. Kate lowered her driver-side window down further, as she drove to work, and enjoyed the breeze on her face. It was a day for a picnic or a trip to the beach, not a day to be stuck in a stuffy office, going over and over the same evidence, trying to find something that would help. *Oh well.* She had the evening with Anderton to look forward to. Immediately her thoughts pinged guiltily to Tin. Did he miss her? Was he regretting his decision?

Are you regretting yours, Kate? She considered it as she swung the car into the station car park and finally decided, with some relief, that she didn't. This thing with Anderton was an added distraction though...but it was such a nice one...

"Kate!" Theo's voice made her jump. "Wake up, woman. It's all kicking off, here."

"What is?" Kate hurriedly tried to pull herself together.

"Melanie Houghton's been arrested again. She's in with Anderton now."

"Oh, he did it then," Kate exclaimed. "Has anything new come in?"

Theo looked puzzled. "Don't think so."

"No new evidence at all?"

"Nope. Not that I'm aware of."

"Oh." Kate reached her desk and sat down, shrugging off her light cardigan. She pushed her hands through her hair and wondered where to begin. "You've heard about Dorothy Smelton, I suppose?"

"Yeah. Poor old cow. Stanton's office emailed to say they'd be doing the PM in a couple of days, but unless something turns up, it's not really our problem."

"No," Kate agreed, but absently. She was feeling that little twist of anxiety that she'd felt for the past few days. You're overwrought, she told herself. Too much emotional turmoil. It's nothing to do with the Farraday case.

Wasn't it? Kate retrieved her notes and began to read through them again. She found the notes of the phone call she'd made yesterday and the answer to the question she'd asked. She leant back in her chair, frowning, and thrust her hands into her pockets, reading and re-reading what she'd written.

There was a twist of paper in her pocket, underneath her fingers. She drew it out and unfolded it, seeing it was the note she'd scribbled herself – a single word – when the thought had occurred to her before. She'd written it two days ago, before she'd gone to see Dorothy for the first time. Poor Dorothy. Kate read the one pencilled word on the scrap of paper. *Trap*. Then she sighed heavily, crumpled it up and threw it onto the surface of her desk. Whatever flash of inspiration she'd had was gone, completely gone.

The morning passed in a blur of paperwork. Kate took a break after several hours and fetched herself a tuna salad and a cup of tea from the station canteen. She was passing by Theo's desk after her lunch when she spotted something in his in-tray that she'd been meaning to have a look at.

"Can I borrow this?" she asked, picking up the flimsy cardboard folder with the logo of the Land Registry stamped upon it.

Theo shrugged. "Be my guest, mate."

"This is all the Farraday property, is it? Or just the town house?"

"It's all of them. I think." Theo yawned. "God, I need a coffee. Want one?"

Kate declined his kind offer and took the folder back to her desk. Leafing through it, she could see her suspicions had been correct. Simon Farraday's name was the only one on all the property deeds.

Was that usual? For all Kate knew, it was a totally legitimate tax fiddle, if that wasn't a contradiction in terms. She needed a lawyer's opinion. Was it worth making a few phone calls? She looked again at the pile of reports awaiting her notice and groaned inwardly. Too much to do and not enough time to do it, and God damn it, why did she feel so uneasy, and what was it that kept bothering her? Kate swore and threw her pen across the room.

"Kate!!" Anderton's shout made her jump. She saw both Chloe and Theo look up at the sound of his voice.

"Sorry, I was just—"

"You could have someone's eye out." Anderton's tone belied his stern words. "Anyway, have you got a minute?"

"Sure." Kate got up and sauntered over to the doorway, as if she didn't have a care in the world. She was impressed with herself. *I should be on the stage,* she thought, marvelling how easy it was to put on an act.

An act... There was another itchy thought there, but the presence of Anderton in his closed-door office drove it away. He didn't kiss her this time but his gaze made it very clear that that was on the cards later.

"So, how about meeting at my club after work? You know where it is, right?"

Kate had eaten there with him before. She approved his choice – it was luxurious and discreet.

"Didn't you say you can get rooms there?" she asked, surprised at her boldness.

Anderton smiled lazily. "I most certainly did."

"Oh, good." Kate wondered whether she had the nerve to reach out and kiss him herself and decided to prolong the delicious anticipation just a little more. "I'll see you there at – what? Seven?"

"Wonderful."

They smiled a complicit goodbye, and Kate left, shutting the door behind her.

*

ANDERTON'S CLUB DID INDEED HAVE rooms for hire, and Kate, sprawled on the bed with him, blissfully entwined, thought it testament to their respective will power that they'd actually managed to have dinner first before making it to bed. They'd already made love once, had a glass of champagne, and were in the preliminary throes of round two when the itch that had been scratching at Kate's brain for the past few days formed itself into a giant, great, pounding fist. Stunned, she let out a gasp very different to the ones she'd just been making and sat bold upright, dislodging Anderton's hands.

"What is it? What's wrong?"

Kate stared at the ceiling, completely dazed. Then she raised both hands to her forehead and fell backwards onto the pillow, still staring upwards. "It's completely meaningless," she said, in an awed tone.

"What?" asked Anderton.

Kate said it again, still looking up at the ceiling. "It's completely meaningless."

The light in the room was dim but she could hear the sudden hurt in his voice. "Meaningless? What? Us? This is? What are you talking about?"

She almost laughed and turned to him, clutching his hands. "No, not *us*. The *alibi*. It's completely meaningless now, can't you see? Oh, God, I can't believe I've only just realised." She let go of his hands and let out her breath in a giant huff. "How could I have only just seen it?"

"Kate Redman, I'm going to spank you in a minute. What the hell are you going on about?"

This time Kate did laugh, half at herself. Shaking her head, she pulled herself into a sitting position and pulled the sheet over herself. She didn't want Anderton to be distracted. *How could I not have seen it before?*

"Listen," said Kate. "It's all so simple. I can't believe I didn't see it before." She could see Anderton start to frown and hurried on. "Listen, I'll tell you all about it. Just sit there and listen to me."

Chapter Twenty-Four

THE GOOD WEATHER HAD GONE by the next day. As Kate sat in the back of Anderton's car, on the way to their destination, she could see the clouds massing in the sky, dark-grey and threatening over the distant hills. As they turned off the main road and began their journey down the winding driveway, the once-fresh green of the trees seemed darker and dulled. The bluebells were over. The illusion of various little lakes reflecting the sky was gone for the year, and the fading flower heads were now shrivelled and brown.

It was a silent journey. Kate, sat in the back and, watching the rear of both Olbeck's and Anderton's heads, began to feel increasingly sick. She didn't believe she'd ever felt so subdued at the thought of making an arrest. That awful sense of foreboding that had dogged her for the past few days was growing stronger. *I wish we didn't have to do this*. But they did, and that was all there was to it.

They parked the car alongside the one belonging to the late master of the house. Kate got out of the car, along with the two men. Her stomach tightened. It was Anderton who rang the doorbell, the two other officers necessarily having to stand behind him because of the narrow path. Kate glanced at the water either side of her. The waterlilies were all in bloom now, delicate white stars sitting atop the water. She swallowed hard as the door began to open.

Mia Farraday looked puzzled but not alarmed at the sight of them. "Good morning—" she began, but Anderton spoke across her.

"We'd like to talk to you, Mrs Farraday."

The graveness of his tone must have given her some clue that this was not a social call. She said nothing, but stepped back to allow them in. Passing her, Kate saw she'd grown even thinner in the time that had passed since her husband's death. Now, Mia was almost frail. Again, Kate's stomach twisted in a nauseous mix of pity and anxiety.

Mia led them through to the living area at the back. There were no Farraday children to be seen, and Kate was, for a moment, so relieved that she didn't question their absence. Then she realised that it was actually a Saturday so they wouldn't have been at school or nursery. She was wondering where they were when Anderton asked the question for her.

"They're out with Sarah," said Mia. Her voice was growing thinner with anxiety. Even so, she began to ask if they wanted tea or coffee, and Anderton, again, spoke over her.

"Do you know why we're here, Mrs Farraday?"

"No," said Mia, but Kate realised that she must have had an inkling of why, because her face didn't change very much as Anderton spoke the words of the caution. It went a little whiter at the mention of the word 'murder' but that was all.

After Anderton had finished speaking, there was a long and awful silence.

"We'd like you to come with us, Mrs Farraday," Anderton said eventually, quite kindly. "We can arrange for you to have legal representation, unless you have someone in mind already."

Mia made a strange, choking noise that Kate, after a moment, identified as a laugh. "No, I don't have someone in mind already."

"Well, perhaps you'll come with us now—" Anderton began but Mia shook her head. Kate could feel Olbeck tense a little beside her, and she braced herself for an escalation of the situation but Mia appeared quite calm.

"I need to sit down for a minute," she said. "I think I might faint."

Kate escorted her to one of the sofas. Mia's arm felt as fragile as a child's. She was wearing a white T-shirt and Kate could feel the coolness of her skin beneath her fingertips, could see the goose bumps rising on Mia's forearm. At the same time, there was a weird kind of energy running through Mia, not quite a trembling but something less tangible. Kate helped her sit down and let her go. She resisted the urge to wipe her hand on her jacket as she stepped back.

Mia dropped her head forwards and took a few deep breaths. Kate could hear how uneven her breathing was.

"Are you all right, Mrs Farraday?" Anderton asked. "Would you like medical assistance?"

Again, Mia gave that strange, choked laugh. "Of course I'm not *all right*." She breathed in and out a few more times. "But I don't need a doctor." She raised her head and fixed her gaze on Anderton. Kate was shocked by the intensity of feeling in her dark eyes. The sense of foreboding screwed a notch tighter.

Mia was speaking again. "I want to know the evidence behind your accusation."

Anderton paused before replying. "What exactly do you mean, Mrs Farraday?"

"I want to know why you think I'm guilty."

The officers exchanged glances. Anderton nodded very slightly at Kate, giving her permission, she hoped, to answer.

She spoke as calmly as she could. "Your alibi for the night of the murder of your husband is meaningless, Mrs Farraday."

Mia looked angry. "What the hell do you mean?"

"I mean, the person who gave you your alibi, Mrs Dorothy Smelton, was suffering from Alzheimer's. She wasn't able to give an accurate time for when you left her house, therefore your alibi is – broken. Destroyed."

Mia half laughed. "That's *it*? That's your evidence?"

She rubbed her temples as if they pained her. "Besides, Dorothy's dead. She died yesterday. So she won't be able to testify, one way or the other."

Kate felt a chill. How did Mia know Dorothy had died? Had somebody told her? Or did she know because...?

"Well, that's interesting," Anderton said in a deceptively casual tone, which immediately told Kate he'd thought the same thing. "I didn't realise you'd heard the news about Mrs Smelton already. That was very quick."

Mia didn't flush. Her face tightened for a moment, and she looked down at the floor. Kate could see her eyelids flickering minutely and had another fanciful thought about Mia, picturing her brain as a lightbulb, an old-fashioned lightbulb, glowing whiter and whiter as the thoughts rushed through her. Whiter and whiter until it shattered, exploded, burst through overload.

Mia looked up and Kate saw her gaze flick up to something over Anderton's shoulder, just for a moment, before she looked away. Then she fixed her gaze once more on Anderton. "I'd like to talk to you. I know – I know you want me to come to the station and I will, but I want to talk here."

"Mrs Farraday—"

"Please. I'll tell you everything. Everything you need to know."

Confession time. Kate had seen it once or twice before, when the weight of guilt suddenly became too much, the peace offered by the act of contrition far outweighing the pain of still keeping the secret. It surprised her though, knowing what she knew about Mia and the lengths the woman had gone to to achieve her aim.

Anderton had perhaps been thinking the same thing. "Very well," he said, and gestured for the other officers to sit down. They did so, keeping a close eye on Mia, but she sat quite still, calm again now. The strange, invisible energy that Kate had sensed about her seemed to have dissipated. "But I must warn you again, Mrs Farraday, that it may harm your defence if you do not mention something which you later rely on in court. Anything you do say may be given in evidence. I just want you to be quite clear on that."

"I understand," said Mia. She looked across at Kate. "It wasn't just the alibi, was it? That can't be the only reason."

Kate didn't smile. "You lied about what you studied at university, Mrs Farraday. You told me that you'd studied History at Edinburgh. You didn't. Your subject was Computer Science, and you had a real aptitude for it, according to your professors. You were one of the top students in your class."

"It's true," Mia said. "I'm highly skilled in computing."

"So I suppose it was child's play for you to hack into your husband's account – no, what am I saying? To hack into Melanie Houghton's account on 4Adults and arrange to meet your husband on the night he was killed?"

Mia stared at Kate. Then she smiled. "You've already examined my computer. I don't believe you found anything suspicious on it."

"Oh, no, not on that one," said Kate, gently. "But that wasn't the one you used, was it Mrs Farraday? Where is your other computer?"

Mia was silent for a long moment. Then she smiled again. "You're not stupid, either, are you DS Redman?"

"The police, despite what you might think, Mrs Farraday, are not stupid."

"No." Mia gave her an appraising stare. "The other computer's hidden behind one of the walls in my bedroom. There's a loose panel behind the dressing table. You can find it there."

"Thank you."

There was a short silence. Kate saw Mia's eyes go beyond Anderton's shoulder once more. What was she looking at? Kate craned her head backwards to try and see but it wasn't obvious. The clock on the wall, perhaps?

"It's true," Mia said. "I killed Simon."

Chapter Twenty-Five

EVEN THOUGH THEY HAD BEEN expecting it, the bald statement caused a faint intake of breath from Olbeck and Kate. Anderton sat calmly. "Why was that?" he asked.

Mia looked down at her hands which were placed flat on either of her narrow thighs. "Well, apart from the fact that he was an awful husband, financially and emotionally abusive, and robbed me of having any more children?" She laughed, properly this time, and for the first time, Kate could detect something not quite sane in her tone. The merest flavour of it, underneath the calm demeanour. "Apart from that?" Her laughter died quite suddenly. "No, that probably wouldn't have been enough. Although..." Suddenly the animation died out of her voice. "Since Mum died, I haven't – things haven't been quite right. With me, I mean." Kate could see her eyelids flickering again, so fast and so faintly it was hard to make out. "He was going to leave me. Leave *us*, more to the point. He'd fallen in love – God, that makes me laugh, Simon in love, he wasn't capable of that, but he thought he was – he was infatuated with that awful woman, and he was just going to up and leave us."

Feeling cruel, but having to ask anyway, Kate said, "But why kill him, Mrs Farraday? Marriages break up all the time."

Mia gave her a look of scorn. "Because I would have had nothing. Literally nothing. He would have seen me and my children in the street, literally in the gutter, with nothing. Penniless. Homeless. Worse, probably." She was silent for a moment and then added, "He was like that."

There was a short silence which Kate opened her mouth to speak before Mia began talking again, in a flat tone that sent another chill down Kate's spine. "Besides, I hated him. I wanted him to die."

What was there to say to that? The officers sat, watching her. Mia, for a moment, seemed oblivious to their stares. She looked down at her hands, still flat on her legs, an oddly dancer-like pose.

Then she looked up. "I did it for the children, you see. They're my life. I'd do anything for them. I *had* to do it."

"Mrs—"Anderton began, but Mia was still speaking.

"It was quite funny, actually. I knew he and that ugly bitch were into all that ridiculous stuff, all the leather and chains and so forth." Her nose wrinkled. "So *cringeworthy*. Her husband must be so humiliated. Well, he should be. Anyway, it was so easy. I knew what the bitch used to wear when she came to see Simon at the townhouse—"

"How did you know?" asked Anderton.

Mia looked at him, surprised. "Because I watched her." She said this as though it were obvious. "I used to spy on her, and her stupid husband, all the time. And Simon too. He genuinely thought I didn't know, or perhaps he did know. He just didn't care." She was silent for a moment and then giggled, a sound that tightened Kate's stomach again. "Sarah thinks I've got loads of hobbies because I was always out. But I don't, really. I just used to go and see what Simon was up to. That's how I knew he was going to leave me and the children. That's how I knew what the bitch wore to meet him. She used to be naked under that raincoat, did you know that? Cheap, nasty slut."

"So you bought the same sort of coat to wear?" asked Kate.

Mia almost looked smug. "Exactly. I set up the meeting, I wore the coat. I knew the police would think it was her."

"You knew about the tunnel," said Kate. Now she realised why Mia hadn't used it to enter the building. She'd wanted to throw suspicion on Melanie Houghton.

"Of course I knew about the tunnel." Mia flexed the fingers of her hands but didn't move from her position. "Anyway, it was easy to persuade Simon to be almost tied-up when I arrived." She giggled again. "I told him to keep the mask on. I said I'd let myself in and he'd have to wait until I'd handcuffed him to the bed properly before I'd take it off. Of course, he agreed. He thought it was Melanie asking him." She was actually laughing now, a thin, gaspy laugh. "God, he got such a shock when he realised it was me."

"He realised?" Kate had thought there hadn't been anything left about this case to shock her but there she realised she was wrong.

Mia was still laughing. "I pulled the mask up, just enough for him to see it was me. I wanted him to know it was me. I wanted him to know that I was onto him. That I'd always been onto him." The thin laughter died. "I meant to kill him but it was supposed to be quite clinical. I don't know what happened. I was—"

She didn't go on. Kate didn't need her to. She could imagine the years of repression and anger and hurt suddenly exploding in one frenzied attack, the candlestick falling again and again and again. She very nearly shuddered. That was why the crime scene had been so contradictory. The long, carefully laid plan *and* the sudden violent attack that took the murderer herself by surprise as much as her victim.

Mia was silent for a long time. So long that Kate could feel Anderton stirring beside her, getting ready to speak.

"Mrs Farraday—"

Mia interrupted him. "I should say that I killed Dorothy, too. Dorothy Smelton." She looked at them a little defiantly, as if she was a naughty schoolgirl, about to be scolded. The officers said nothing but looked back. Mia went on. "I'm not ashamed of that. I'm not ashamed of killing Simon either, actually. I'm just sorry it had to be so – so messy. But Dorothy – it was what she wanted. She told me."

Kate could see Anderton, seasoned officer as he was, struggling to make sense of that. "She *told* you—"

Mia spoke quite coolly. "Dorothy was very ill. She had Alzheimer's, I'm sure you already know that. I knew it, quite early on. Having been through it all with Mum, I knew very early on. I knew the signs, you see." She fell silent for a moment, and for the first time, Kate saw tears in her eyes. "Dorothy had seen what I'd gone through with Mum. I remember she said to me once, 'I don't want to end up like that, Mia. I want to be put out of my misery before it gets too bad'."

The officers said nothing. Kate thought what Mia was saying was probably true. Dorothy's words to her on her first visit to the lady's house reoccurred, something about it being okay to put animals down but not people. She realised Mia was speaking again.

"I knew Dorothy wouldn't know what time I actually left her, that night. The night Simon was killed. I told her what to say. I reminded her." Mia blinked again, rapidly. "She called me yesterday morning, terribly upset. She was paranoid about the police, she thought they were trying to break into her house. I said I'd go over there." She sighed. "I knew as soon as I saw her that it was – it was time. Time to do what I'd said I'd do."

"Nothing to do with the fact that she was becoming more and more unreliable," said Anderton, and this time his tone was not gentle or neutral. "Nothing to do with the fact that she could have betrayed you to the police."

"No," said Mia, dully. "It wasn't like that."

"So, what happened?"

"I gave her pills. In brandy. She didn't know anything was happening. She died peacefully."

There was another long silence. Kate wondered whether Anderton would break it, by insisting Mia Farraday now accompany them to the station. She was sure he was about to, when they were all startled by the sound of the front door opening and then the noise and hubbub of several small children approaching the kitchen. A moment later, Sarah Collins and two of the Farraday children entered the room.

*

FOR A MOMENT, ALL THREE officers and Mia Farraday sat as if turned to stone. Kate, heart beating fast, wondered whether Anderton would say anything. The two small children, little Tilly and a slightly older boy who must have been Milo, made a rush towards their mother, only to stop at the sight of the three strange adults sat silently on the opposite sofa.

Mia was the first one to break the silence. "Where's James?"

Sarah Collins came forward into the living area from the kitchen. She was obviously sensitive enough to be aware of the tension that filled the room. "What's the matter?"

Mia ignored her question. "Where's James?"

Sarah glanced from Mia to the police officers nervously. "He – we ran into his friend Toby, and James wanted to go and play at his house. I said I thought that would be okay. I'll go and fetch him in an hour or so."

"No!" The agony in Mia's voice brought them all up short. Tilly put her thumb in her mouth, her face puckering. "He has to be *here*! We all need to be together."

"I'm sorry." Sarah Collins was almost in tears herself, the knowledge that something was terribly wrong obviously hitting her hard. "I can go and get him, right now."

Mia stilled suddenly. She froze, her face a blank, neutral mask. In her mind's eye, Kate saw the image of the glowing lightbulb again, the sizzle and pop as the connection overloaded, the sudden extinction of the light.

Very slowly, Mia smiled. Or if not smiled, stretched the corners of her mouth sideways. "It doesn't matter," she said in a monotone. "No, it doesn't matter. James is old enough to cope."

They all stared at her. Mia shook herself slightly and addressed Anderton. "I'm ready to come with you now, Inspector. But I must be allowed to say goodbye to my children first."

The knot in Kate's stomach was growing. She saw the sceptical look on Anderton's face.

"That's fine, Mrs Farraday, as long as you make it quick."

"I meant, in private."

Kate saw Anderton look at Mia. "No. I'm sorry but I can't allow that."

Mia's face contracted. "*Please*. Let me say my goodbyes with some – some dignity."

"No, Mrs Farraday. I'm afraid not."

"Oh—"

Anderton relented slightly "I will allow you to talk to your children in this room. You can take them over to that corner if you like." He nodded towards the far wall. "But you will not be allowed to leave this room. I'm sorry, but that's final."

Mia obviously realised that he couldn't be moved. She didn't say anything but her face grew a little whiter. She was now so pale that with her hollowed cheekbones, and the shadows beneath her eyes, for a moment her face resembled a skull. She crouched down and held her arms out to her children. "Come here, darlings. Come with Mummy."

Kate watched her lead them over to the far side of the room, past the breakfast bar of the kitchen that edged the side of the living area. She thought she saw Mia's pale arm flicker out for a moment but she was distracted in the next instance by Anderton murmuring to her and Olbeck that enough was enough and it was time to bring Mia Farraday in, children or no children.

"Well, I think—" Olbeck said, but they never got to hear what it was he thought because in the next instance, Kate's stomach contracted as if she'd suddenly been kicked by a horse, and the next second she was racing, racing across the room, leaping over the back of the sofa, just as the scream exited from Tilly's little mouth. Kate hit the floor heavily – stumbled, righted herself – and cannoned into Mia just as she was raising the knife for the second time, the knife she'd just taken from the knife block on the breakfast bar. There was a second of confused scrimmage, of blood arcing up over the room – Kate felt the warm spray of it as it hit her face – but she didn't know who was hit or who was hurt. Mia was panting, the little girl and boy were screaming, and then there was a black-edged maelstrom of panic and fear and confusion.

"No, Mia, no, Mia!" Kate heard herself shouting as she struggled with Mia for possession of the knife. "No, no, don't—"

Mia's thin body belied her strength. She pushed Kate away, but as Kate stumbled back, she managed to grab hold of both the children, both frozen with fear.

Kate flung them both backwards, not caring if they hurt themselves in the fall, just frantic to get them out of Mia's reach. Mia screamed. Then, before anyone could do anything, before Olbeck and Anderton could reach her, she gave her children one last, despairing glance and turned her back on them all. Kate saw her hand rise and the knife describe one shining sweep in the air but the blood that flew out was hidden from the children's view, just as Mia would have planned it, as she'd planned everything else.

Chapter Twenty-Six

IT WAS EARLY EVENING BY the time Kate was finally discharged from the Accident and Emergency department at Abbeyford Hospital. Both Anderton and Olbeck were sitting in the waiting room as she finally emerged from the ward, both slumped in the uncomfortable plastic chairs. Kate, walking wearily towards them, thought that if there were a less flattering light than the strip lights found in hospital waiting areas, then she had yet to find it.

Anderton was the first to spot her and jumped up. "Are you—" he began, but Kate was already talking over him.

"What's the news on Tilly Farraday?"

"She'll be okay," said Anderton, and Kate nearly swooned with relief. She limped over to the row of plastic chairs and flopped down in one. Olbeck sat next to her and put his arm around her which, in her tired state, caused Kate some confusion because shouldn't it be Anderton who was comforting her?

Then she snapped back to reality and gave her friend a grateful smile.

"Thank God Tilly's going to be okay," she said. Then, hating to ask but having to know, she said in a more subdued tone, "What about Mia?"

The two men exchanged glances before Anderton answered, and in that time, Kate could feel her stomach begin to drop. She held her breath.

"She's still in Intensive Care," Anderton said sombrely. "It's touch and go, from what I understand. She lost a hell of a lot of blood."

"Well, that's what happens when you cut your own throat," Kate said, dimly aware of how callous that sounded. But then it had been she who had ridden in the ambulance with Tilly Farraday, she who had held the little girl's hand and seen the naked terror in her eyes. Desperate as Mia Farraday had been, nothing could excuse putting her child through that.

"Surely she didn't always mean to kill them," said Olbeck. He sounded tired.

"Of course not," said Kate. "She did this all for them. But when it came down to it, in the end, she wasn't going to leave them. I suppose she thought better that they all go together. If she was capable of thinking anything, by the end."

"Yes." Olbeck pondered for a moment, removing his arm from Kate's shoulders. "I wonder if she'll plead insanity?"

Anderton shook his head but without anger. "Not

likely. Whatever her state of mind at the end, the whole – campaign, I suppose you'd call it – showed a level of calculation and planning that I personally find quite staggering." He sighed. "She was clever. Very clever."

"What put you onto her, Kate?" Olbeck asked. Kate realised, with dull surprise, that they'd not even had a chance to discuss the case since the revelation of Mia's guilt.

"Oh, it was a remark of Dorothy Smelton's." She eased back in her chair and contemplated her bandaged forearms. Whilst Kate had not been badly injured, it had been Sarah Collins' quick action in calling an ambulance that had saved Tilly Farraday and (hopefully) Mia Farraday too. Whilst Kate, Olbeck and Anderton had been grappling with Mia, trying to stem the arterial flow of blood from her slashed neck, Sarah Collins had coolly administered first aid to the injured Tilly, soothed her screaming brother and calmly directed the ambulances to the house. Kate forgave her for sleeping with Simon Farraday, which is indeed what had happened; Sarah had tearfully confessed all on the way to the hospital.

"Which was?"

Kate had been leaning back with closed eyes. She opened them with some difficulty. Adrenaline was finally wearing off, and she felt as if a twelve-hour sleep would probably not be quite enough to restore her. "What? Oh. Yes. Dorothy said something about

Mia's degree subject – something Mia had excelled in, apparently, I mean really excelled in, almost to the point of being a minor genius – anyway, Dorothy said something about not understanding 'all that new-fangled stuff'. And Mia had told me she'd done History, so that just didn't make sense."

"That was *it*?"

"Well, to start with," admitted Kate. "But it niggled me. It irked me. So I double checked with Edinburgh University and found out that she'd actually studied computing. That was puzzling, but it didn't really seem to have any bearing on the case until after Dorothy's death, when the whole question of Mia's alibi was called into question."

"We should have seen it before," Anderton said gloomily. "We should have done a more thorough search, for one thing."

Neither of the other two said anything. After a moment, Olbeck's mobile chimed with an incoming text. He pulled it out of his pocket and read it.

"That's Jeff, he's coming to pick me up. Kate, do you want us to drop you home?"

Kate wavered. Part of her was desperate to get home and get some sleep. But the other half of her was very conscious of the fact that Anderton was here, right here beside her, and she didn't want to leave him. "Well—"

"That's all right," Anderton said suddenly. "I'll drop Kate home. Don't make Jeff go out of his way unnecessarily."

Kate wondered whether Olbeck would find this a little suspicious but he was obviously too tired to read anything into it. He yawned and said, "Rightio, then, I'll be off." He kissed Kate on the cheek, shook Anderton's hand, and made his way outside. Kate, watching him go, thought that she must talk to him soon and tell him how things were with Anderton. She didn't want there to be any secrets between them. But then, how could she tell Olbeck how things were with Anderton when she wasn't sure herself?

As if he'd read her mind, Anderton leant over and helped her to her feet. "Come on, DS Redman. I think I promised to wine and dine you tonight, hadn't I?"

Kate glanced at him, her mouth turning up at the corners. "What about the last part to that well known saying?"

"If I have the energy."

Kate laughed. Feeling light-hearted, despite her tiredness and the sting of the cuts on her arms, she took Anderton's hand, feeling as if life and warmth and energy were flowing back into her from the touch of his fingers in hers. They walked out into the spring night together.

THE END

ENJOYED THIS BOOK? AN HONEST review left at Amazon and Goodreads is always welcome and *really* important for indie authors. The more reviews an independently published book has, the easier it is to market it and find new readers.

Want some more of Celina Grace's work for free? Subscribers to her mailing list get a free digital copy of **Requiem (A Kate Redman Mystery: Book 2)**, a free digital copy of **A Prescription for Death (The Asharton Manor Mysteries Book 2)** *and* a free PDF copy of her short story collection **A Blessing From The Obeah Man.**

Requiem (A Kate Redman Mystery: Book 2)

WHEN THE BODY OF TROUBLED teenager Elodie Duncan is pulled from the river in Abbeyford, the case is at first assumed to be a straightforward suicide. Detective Sergeant Kate Redman is shocked to discover that she'd met the victim the night before her death, introduced by Kate's younger brother Jay. As the case develops, it becomes clear that Elodie was murdered. A talented young musician, Elodie had been keeping some strange company and was hiding her own dark secrets.

As the list of suspects begin to grow, so do the questions. What is the significance of the painting Elodie modelled for? Who is the man who was seen with her on the night of her death? Is there any connection with another student's death at the exclusive musical college that Elodie attended?

As Kate and her partner Detective Sergeant Mark Olbeck attempt to unravel the mystery, the dark undercurrents of the case threaten those whom Kate holds most dear...

A Prescription for Death (The Asharton Manor Mysteries: Book 2) – a novella

"I HAD A SURGE OF KINSHIP the first time I saw the manor, perhaps because we'd both seen better days."

It is 1947. Asharton Manor, once one of the most beautiful stately homes in the West Country, is now a convalescent home for former soldiers. Escaping the devastation of post-war London is Vivian Holt, who moves to the nearby village and begins to volunteer as a nurse's aide at the manor. Mourning the death of her soldier husband, Vivian finds solace in her new friendship with one of the older patients, Norman Winter, someone who has served his country in both world wars. Slowly, Vivian's heart begins to heal, only to be torn apart when she arrives for work one day to be told that Norman is dead.

It seems a straightforward death, but is it? Why did a particular photograph disappear from Norman's possessions after his death? Who is the sinister figure who keeps following Vivian? Suspicion and doubts begin to grow and when another death occurs, Vivian begins to realise that the war may be over but the real battle is just beginning...

A Blessing From The Obeah Man

DARE YOU READ ON? HORRIFYING, scary, sad and thought-provoking, this short story collection will take you on a macabre journey. In the titular story, a honeymooning couple take a wrong turn on their trip around Barbados. The Mourning After brings you a shivery story from a suicidal teenager. In Freedom Fighter, an unhappy middle-aged man chooses the wrong day to make a bid for freedom, whereas Little Drops of Happiness and Wave Goodbye are tales of darkness from sunny Down Under. Strapping Lass and The Club are for those who prefer, shall we say, a little meat to the story...

JUST GO TO CELINA'S WEBSITE www.celinagrace. com to sign up. It's quick, easy and free. Be the first to be informed of promotions, giveaways, new releases and subscriber-only benefits by subscribing to her (occasional) newsletter.

Aspiring or new authors might like to check out Celina's other site www.indieauthorschool.com for motivation, inspiration and advice on writing and publishing a book, or even starting a whole new career as an indie author. Get a free eBook, a mini e-course, cheat sheets and other helpful downloads when you sign up for the newsletter.

www.celinagrace.com
www.indieauthorschool.com
Twitter: @celina__grace
Pinterest: Indie_Author_School
Facebook: www.facebook.com/authorcelinagrace

More books by Celina Grace...

Hushabye (A Kate Redman Mystery: Book 1)

ON THE FIRST DAY OF her new job in the West Country, Detective Sergeant Kate Redman finds herself investigating the kidnapping of Charlie Fullman, the newborn son of a wealthy entrepreneur and his trophy wife. It seems a straightforward case... but as Kate and her fellow officer Mark Olbeck delve deeper, they uncover murky secrets and multiple motives for the crime.

Kate finds the case bringing up painful memories of her own past secrets. As she confronts the truth about herself, her increasing emotional instability threatens both her hard-won career success and the possibility that they will ever find Charlie Fullman alive...

Hushabye is the book that introduces
Detective Sergeant Kate Redman.
Available as a FREE download from Amazon Kindle.

Imago (A Kate Redman Mystery: Book 3)

"THEY DON'T FEAR ME, QUITE the opposite. It makes it twice as fun... I know the next time will be soon, I've learnt to recognise the signs. I think I even know who it will be. She's oblivious of course, just as she should be. All the time, I watch and wait and she has no idea, none at all. And why would she? I'm disguised as myself, the very best disguise there is."

A known prostitute is found stabbed to death in a shabby corner of Abbeyford. Detective Sergeant Kate Redman and her partner Detective Sergeant Olbeck take on the case, expecting to have it wrapped up in a matter of days. Kate finds herself distracted by her growing attraction to her boss, Detective Chief Inspector Anderton – until another woman's body is found, with the same knife wounds. And then another one after that, in a matter of days.

Forced to confront the horrifying realisation that a serial killer may be preying on the vulnerable women of Abbeyford, Kate, Olbeck and the team find themselves in a race against time to unmask a terrifying murderer, who just might be hiding in plain sight...

Available now from Amazon.

Snarl (A Kate Redman Mystery: Book 4)

A RESEARCH LABORATORY OPENS ON the outskirts of Abbeyford, bringing with it new people, jobs, prosperity and publicity to the area – as well as a mob of protesters and animal rights activists. The team at Abbeyford police station take this new level of civil disorder in their stride – until a fatal car bombing of one of the laboratory's head scientists means more drastic measures must be taken...

Detective Sergeant Kate Redman is struggling to come to terms with being back at work after long period of absence on sick leave; not to mention the fact that her erstwhile partner Olbeck has now been promoted above her. The stakes get even higher as a multiple murder scene is uncovered and a violent activist is implicated in the crime. Kate and the team must put their lives on the line to expose the murderer and untangle the snarl of accusations, suspicions and motives.

Available now from Amazon.

Chimera (A Kate Redman Mystery: Book 5)

THE WEST COUNTRY TOWN OF Abbeyford is celebrating its annual pagan festival, when the festivities are interrupted by the discovery of a very decomposed body. Soon, several other bodies are discovered but is it a question of foul play or are these deaths from natural causes?

It's a puzzle that Detective Sergeant Kate Redman and the team could do without, caught up as they are in investigating an unusual series of robberies. Newly single again, Kate also has to cope with her upcoming Inspector exams and a startling announcement from her friend and colleague DI Mark Olbeck...

When a robbery goes horribly wrong, Kate begins to realise that the two cases might be linked. She must use all her experience and intelligence to solve a serious of truly baffling crimes which bring her up against an old adversary from her past...

Available now from Amazon.

Echo (A Kate Redman Mystery: Book 6)

THE WEST COUNTRY TOWN OF Abbeyford is suffering its worst floods in living memory when a landslide reveals the skeletal remains of a young woman. Detective Sergeant Kate Redman is assigned to the case but finds herself up against a baffling lack of evidence, missing files and the suspicion that someone on high is blocking her investigation...

Matters are complicated by her estranged mother making contact after years of silence. As age-old secrets are uncovered and powerful people are implicated, Kate and the team are determined to see justice done. But at what price?

Available now from Amazon.

Creed (A Kate Redman Mystery: Book 7)

JOSHUA WIDCOMBE AND KAYA TRENT were the golden couple of Abbeyford's School of Art and Drama; good-looking, popular and from loving, stable families. So why did they kill themselves on the grassy stage of the college's outdoor theatre?

Detective Chief Inspector Anderton thinks there might be something more to the case than a straightforward teenage suicide pact. Detective Sergeant Kate Redman agrees with him, but nothing is certain until another teenager at the college kills herself, quickly followed by yet another death. Why are the privileged teens of this exclusive college killing themselves? Is this a suicide cluster?

As Kate and the team delve deeper into the case, secrets and lies rear their ugly heads and Abbeyford CID are about to find out that sometimes, the most vulnerable people can be the most deadly...

Available now from Amazon.

Sanctuary (A Kate Redman Mystery: Book 8)

Dawn breaks at Muddiford Beach and the body of a young African man is discovered lying on the sand. Was he a desperate asylum seeker, drowned in his attempt to reach the safe shores of Britain? Or is there a more sinister explanation for his death?

Irritated to discover that the investigation will be a joint one with the neighbouring police force at Salterton CID, Detective Sergeant Kate Redman is further annoyed by her Salterton counterpart, one of the rudest young women Kate has ever encountered.

Tensions rise as the two teams investigate the case and when a second body is discovered, Kate and her colleagues are to about realise just how far people will go in the cause of doing good...

Available now from Amazon.

Valentine (A Kate Redman Mystery Novella)

A RESPECTABLE, MIDDLE-AGED HOUSEWIFE. AN AMBITIOUS young lawyer. A student burlesque dancer. Three women with nothing in common – except for the fact that someone has sent them a macabre Valentine's Day gift; a pig's heart pierced by an arrow.

Is this a case of serious harm intended? Or just a malicious prank? Detective Inspector Olbeck thinks there might be something more sinister behind it but his colleague Detective Sergeant Kate Redman is too busy mourning the departure of her partner Tin to New York to worry too much about the case. Until one of the women receives a death threat...

Available now from Amazon.

CELINA GRACE'S PSYCHOLOGICAL THRILLER, **LOST Girls** is also available from Amazon:

Twenty-three years ago, Maudie Sampson's childhood friend Jessica disappeared on a family holiday in Cornwall. She was never seen again.

In the present day, Maudie is struggling to come to terms with the death of her wealthy father, her increasingly fragile mental health and a marriage that's under strain. Slowly, she becomes aware that there is someone following her: a blonde woman in a long black coat with an intense gaze. As the woman begins to infiltrate her life, Maudie realises no one else appears to be able to see her.

Is Maudie losing her mind? Is the woman a figment of her imagination or does she actually exist? Have the sins of the past caught up with Maudie's present... or is there something even more sinister going on?

Lost Girls is a novel from the author of **The House on Fever Street**: a dark and convoluted tale which proves that nothing can be taken for granted and no-one is as they seem.

Available now from Amazon.

THE HOUSE ON FEVER STREET is the first psychological thriller by **Celina Grace**.

Thrown together in the aftermath of the London bombings of 2005, Jake and Bella embark on a passionate and intense romance. Soon Bella is living with Jake in his house on Fever Street, along with his sardonic brother Carl and Carl's girlfriend, the beautiful but chilly Veronica.

As Bella tries to come to terms with her traumatic experience, her relationship with Jake also becomes a source of unease. Why do the housemates never go into the garden? Why does Jake have such bad dreams and such explosive outbursts of temper?

Bella is determined to understand the man she loves but as she uncovers long-buried secrets, is she putting herself back into mortal danger?

The House on Fever Street is the first psychological thriller from writer Celina Grace – a chilling study of the violent impulses that lurk beneath the surfaces of everyday life.

Shortlisted for the 2006 Crime Writers' Association Debut Dagger Award.

Available now from Amazon.

EXTRA SPECIAL THANKS ARE DUE TO MY WONDERFUL ADVANCE READERS TEAM...

THESE ARE MY 'SUPER READERS' who are kind enough to beta read my books, point out my more ridiculous mistakes, spot any typos that have slipped past my editor and best of all, write honest reviews in exchange for advance copies of my work. Many, many thanks to you all.

If you fancy being an Advance Reader, just drop me a line at celina@celinagrace.com and I'll add you to the list. It's completely free, and you can unsubscribe at any time.

ACKNOWLEDGEMENTS

MANY THANKS TO ALL THE following splendid souls:

Chris Howard for the brilliant cover designs; Andrea Harding for editing and proofreading; Tammi Lebrecque for virtual assistance; lifelong Schlockers and friends David Hall, Ben Robinson and Alberto Lopez; Ross McConnell for advice on police procedural and for also being a great brother; Kathleen and Pat McConnell, Anthony Alcock, Naomi White, Mo Argyle, Lee Benjamin, Bonnie Wede, Sherry and Amali Stoute, Cheryl and Mark Beckles, Georgia Lucas-Going, Steven Lucas, Loletha Stoute and Harry Lucas, Helen Parfect, Helen Watson, Emily Way, Sandy Hall, Kristýna Vosecká, Katie D'Arcy and of course my wonderful and ever-loving Chris, Mabel, Jethro and Isaiah.

Printed in Great Britain
by Amazon